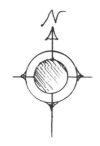

STONEWALL'S GOLD

Robert J. Mrazek

STONEWALL'S GOLD

A NOVEL

Robert J. Mrazek

ST. MARTIN'S PRESS
NEW YORK

THOMAS DUNNE BOOKS.
An imprint of St. Martin's Press.

Maps by Martie Holmer

Production Editor: David Stanford Burr

Library of Congress Cataloging-in-Publication Data

Mrazek, Robert J.
    Stonewall's gold : a novel / Robert J. Mrazek. — 1st ed.
      p.   cm.
    ISBN 0-312-20024-2
    1. Shenandoah River Valley (Va. and W. Va.)—History—Civil War, 1861–1865—Fiction. 2. Virginia—History—Civil War, 1861–1865—Fiction. I. Title.
PS3563.R39S76   1999
813'.54—dc21   98-36891
                                                 CIP

First Edition: January 1999

10 9 8 7 6 5 4 3 2 1

For Cathie, Susannah, and James, with love.

The War of the Rebellion:
The Official Records of the Union and Confederate Armies.
Volume 40, Part 3, Page 223.

City Point, Virginia
July 14, 1864

By Order of Ulysses S. Grant, Lieutenant General:

"If the enemy has left Maryland, as I suppose he has, he should have upon his heels veterans, militiamen, men on horseback, and everything that can be got to follow to eat out Virginia clear and clean as far as they go, so that crows flying over it for the balance of this season will have to carry their provender with them."

Mrs. Edmund I. Lee to General David Hunter

Shepherdstown, Virginia
July 20, 1864

General Hunter,

Yesterday morning, your underling, Capt. Martindale of the First New York Veteran Cavalry, executed your infamous order and burned my house: the dwelling and outbuildings seven in number with all their contents. I therefore, a helpless woman whom you have cruelly wronged, address you a Major General of the United States Army and demand, why was this done? What was my offense?

The house was built by my father, a Revolutionary patriot who served the whole seven years for your independence. There was I born. There the sacred dead repose . . . and there has your niece, who lived among us all this horrid war up to the present, met with all kindness and hospitality at my hands.

Can I say "God forgive you?" Were it possible for human lips to raise your name heavenward, angels would thrust the foul thing back. The curses of thousands, the scorn of the manly and upright and the hatred of the true and honorable will follow you and yours through all time.

Explanatory Note

THE FOLLOWING MANUSCRIPT was discovered in the archives of the Rockingham County courthouse in Harrisonburg, Virginia. Apparently, it was part of a docket filed in 1865 by Judge Francis Channing Burwell, who, as Civil War scholars are well aware, served with great distinction as a combat commander in the fabled 2nd Virginia Regiment under Lieutenant General Thomas Jonathan "Stonewall" Jackson, and then later as a staff officer to Lieutenant General Jubal A. Early.

A graduate of the University of Virginia, Colonel Burwell went on to enjoy a long and distinguished career as a jurist of the Virginia Appellate Court, dying at the age of ninety-one while "taking the waters" in Orkney Springs, Virginia.

For reasons never publicly disclosed by the judge, the docket was sealed from public scrutiny for a period of fifty years. Thereafter, the documents remained buried in the court archives until they were found by a student at Bridgewater College during the course of her research into the life and wartime exploits of the "Fighting Judge."

The manuscript depicts a savage and sometimes barbarous time in the Shenandoah Valley during the final weeks of the Civil War. It was a dramatically different period from those early days of the fighting when Union and Confederate soldiers were known to succor their wounded enemy and exchange coffee for tobacco across the lines.

For readers unfamiliar with the Shenandoah Valley, it is a

place of sheer breathtaking beauty. More than a hundred miles long from north to south, its pastoral fields and meadows are bordered to the west by the "Mighty Alleghenies," and to the east by the Blue Ridge Mountains. Running straight down the middle is the forbidding and craggy Massanutten.

It was here in the spring of 1862 that Stonewall Jackson embarked on one of the most brilliant campaigns in the history of warfare. Leading a force that never totaled more than 17,000 men, he marched his "foot cavalry" 650 miles in six weeks, eventually defeating five separate Union armies with an aggregate strength more than triple his own. His final victory was achieved at Port Republic on June 9, 1862, after which he went on to enduring fame.

Throughout the Civil War, the Shenandoah Valley served as a rich store of grain and livestock for Lee's Army of Northern Virginia. In the summer of 1864, Lieutenant General Ulysses S. Grant decided to eliminate the valley as a source of supply.

Union Major General Philip H. Sheridan inherited the task of executing Grant's infamous order of July 14. For months thereafter he waged a systematic campaign of destruction against the defenseless civilian population.

In his official report of October 5, Major General Wesley Merritt, commanding just one of Sheridan's divisions, stated that his troops alone were responsible for destroying 630 well-stocked barns, 47 mills, 410,742 bushels of wheat, and 515 acres of corn, not including private dwellings and livestock. By the time the Union Army was finished, the once picturesque landscape was "a scene of deserted homesteads, smouldering ruins, wasted fields, shattered groves and general desolation."

The last bitter winter before General Lee surrendered his army was thus a time of hardship and deprivation in the Shenandoah Valley. After four years of carnage, all traces of civility had disappeared. A spirit of vengefulness led to a level of malevolent behavior on both sides which was often random and sudden. Deserters and other desperate men roamed the valley at will, often preying on innocent citizens. Violence permeated the land.

STONEWALL'S GOLD

ONE

CONSTABLE KILDUFF has told me to put the whole thing down in writing and that is exactly what I'm going to do. He said if I could offer enough evidence to prove it really happened the way I said it did then everything would come out all right in the end. He said he thought Judge Burwell would not go hard on a fifteen-year-old boy, even for the murders.

When I'm finished writing it all down, he'll take it to the judge over at the courthouse in Harrisonburg. After that, Constable Kilduff said I would likely be able to start life again with a clean slate.

Don't ask me why this happened to me. My mother said it was part of God's plan. If it was, I'd say He needs a lot more practice. Anyway, it all started in those last few months before General Lee surrendered at Appamatox.

Jubal Early and his Shenandoah army were finished once and for all in the valley. A week after they got whipped by the Yankees for the last time at Cedar Creek, a long train of hospital wagons arrived in Port Republic and the wounded were laid out on piles of straw around Fairfield Hall. My mother and the other women went over there to help ease their pain and try to comfort the dying.

Now those men were gone too. A lot of them were buried in the same fields around the hall. Most of the others had slipped across the Blue Ridge through Brown's Gap to join General Lee for a last stand around Richmond and Petersburg.

General Sheridan had sent his cavalry raiding up the valley again in late October. They swarmed all over like locusts until that great leader finally figured out there was nobody left to bother with. Of course, that didn't stop them from burning or destroying almost everything in their path for the pure pleasure it gave them.

On the day I turned fifteen, they came to our place. After piling straw around the barn, the soldiers drove our two milk cows inside, shut the doors and set it on fire. Then they killed the chickens and stole all the cured meat from the smokehouse. They were very good at their job. The whole matter took less than ten minutes.

We had our first hoarfrost a few days later. By late November the ice in Dorsey's pond was already four inches thick and people were saying it was the coldest winter they could ever remember. In mid-December we began having fierce storms almost every day with snow squalls and ice rain.

It wasn't much past four o'clock on the afternoon the stranger came. The sky was already turning dark. With another bitter night coming on I was making sure our last horse, Jupiter, was safely bedded down in the run-in shed near the back of our house.

That's when Achilles began to growl. The big mastiff was so old that his muzzle had turned milky-white but his ears were still fine. I turned to look down the hill toward the woods and saw him riding up out of the gloom.

His animal was making an ugly snuffling noise like it wasn't too happy to be out on such a miserable day. When he reached the top of the hill, the stranger rode slowly across the yard to the hitching post near the back porch. He never looked in my direction although Jupiter whinnied out a friendly greeting as they went by. Dismounting, he tied up his horse.

His head was covered by a high-crowned beaver hat and he wore a long military greatcoat with its collars turned up to protect his ears from the cold. The insignia had been ripped off but I knew it was an officer's coat because my father was wearing one just like it when they brought him home after he was shot at Chancellorsville.

A short-barreled carbine hung across the stranger's back, held on by a crude strap that ran from his right shoulder down to his left hip. What looked like cowhide breeches were stuffed into long cavalry boots. He must have been wearing spurs because they made an odd jangling sound with every step he took up to the back porch. He knocked loudly twice on the kitchen door.

When my mother answered it, he said, "They told me in the village you had room, Miz Lockhart." His voice was loud enough to carry over the wind. It was deep and grizzly.

I couldn't hear her answer but the next thing I saw he was heading inside. A few minutes later I walked over to look at his horse. It was short, stubby, and narrow-chested, about the only kind you saw anymore in the valley since General Hunter's bummers had come through back in the summer and stolen everything that wasn't nailed down. Aside from his satchel bag, the only thing the stranger's horse was carrying was a corked jug that hung from a length of twine tied to the pommel of his saddle.

I know my mother would never have rented him our room if we weren't so hard up for the extra money. Not that it was any palace. When my grandfather built his fruit cellar into the side of the hill behind the house, he constructed a large room above it with a second-story loft. For years it was used as a place to store tools. Later, my father fixed it up as an office before he began teaching at the Mossy Creek Academy.

My mother started renting it after the Yankees captured Winchester for the first time and prices at the store right away doubled for just about everything. Our first boarder was an old widower whose house took fire during the fighting at Tenth Legion. He stayed with us for almost a year until his daughter came up from Kentucky to get him. After that it was a mixed trade. Most of them were bargemen who had brought freight goods up the river and then got stuck in Port Republic when the fighting blocked their passage any further.

As far as I was concerned we didn't need any more boarders now. No matter what the old men said down at the store I knew in my heart the war couldn't last much longer and my father would be coming home again soon. I couldn't wait for things to be just like they used to be.

I finished currying Jupiter and headed inside. After hanging up my coat, I went through the back pantry into the kitchen. The stranger was sitting in my father's chair in front of the fire. He had removed his hat and coat to reveal a filthy red shirt covered by a rawhide vest that was held together by a leather watch chain. I saw that the sole of one of his boots was sprung wide open and he wasn't wearing any socks. But that wasn't unusual. Dr. Cassidy had said more than half the Confederate soldiers were completely barefoot.

He was by far the hairiest man I've ever seen. The roots started growing out of his forehead just above the brows of his fearsome black eyes. Like some kind of pelt it rose straight back over the crown of his head and fell way down below his shoulders. It even sprouted out of the backs of his hands. There were tiny icicles frozen into the long black beard that began just below his lips.

My mother was telling him exactly what I had hoped to

hear. It was what she always said when she didn't like the looks of someone who asked to stay.

"My husband is away at the moment but we've received word that he is on his way home. We expect him to arrive any day now. I regret that he is usually accompanied by another officer who will have need of our spare room."

At this the stranger broke into a smile that shattered the ice particles covering his chin. I'll say this for him. He still had all his teeth.

"I reckon I cain understand that," he said. " 'Course, I don't need it for mor'n a week at most. If'n your husband come home I'd get right out for sure. Don't want to get in the way of no homecomin' party. No, sir. I just wisht I had somebody waitin' for me at home after all I been through. Now I was with the artillery myself. Back in sixty-two I fought right here under ol' Stonewall hisself. Right across them fields yonder," he said, pointing in the direction of the battlefield.

"Well, I'm truly sorry but—"

"Ma'arm, I surely would like a place with a real bed. I'll pay three hundred dollars the week if'n you let me stay. How's that sound?"

Of course, he was talking Confederate. Three hundred was barely enough to buy a good pair of pants but it was five times what she would have usually asked and I could see she was already spending the money in her mind on things we needed to last out the winter.

Then he said, " 'Course, I'll get out the first minute your husbin come walkin' through that door."

I was about to ask him what was so special about any old bed in Port Republic when I heard my mother tell him, "If we have to ask you to leave, I will return the unused portion of the rent. And you're welcome to take meals with us although I'm afraid there isn't much to put on the table these days."

"That's mighty kind of you, ma'arm," he said.

"You'll find a pitcher and bowl on the washstand in your room and the pump is in the well house by the side porch," she went on. I doubted he would soon be taking her up on that knowledge. His fingernails were caked with dirt and he looked like he hadn't washed in a month.

"The necessary can be found in the grove of black walnuts beyond the run-in shed."

"Yes, ma'arm," he said, looking around at everything as if he now owned the place. "My name's Blewitt. Corporal Blewitt."

The black eyes stopped on me and his nose curdled up as if he smelled something bad. I figured it was probably himself.

"An' how old are you, boy?" he demanded.

"Fifteen."

"Fifteen!" he repeated, making his eyes go wide. "Mite small, ain't you?"

I said nothing in return. It was regrettably true. My mother always said, "God may have made you small so far, Jamie, but he also gave you common sense and a good brain." Personally, I'd give a good chunk of it back to Him if He would make me around six feet tall.

"I'll say this," Corporal Blewitt added. "You as pretty as a girl."

My face got hot and I was about to take his and the Lord's name in vain when my mother said, "Jamie, please go tend to Corporal Blewitt's horse while I finish preparing supper."

"Mighty obliged, ma'arm," he said.

Putting on my coat again in the pantry, I was about to walk out the door when I heard him say, "They tell me you a Yankee lady."

There was a pause and then she replied as if all the life had gone out of her.

"Who told you that?" she asked.

"Fat boy runs the store."

6

"I'm originally from New York," she said so low I could barely hear. "I've lived here for sixteen years."

I went outside and led his mare back to the run-in shed. She seemed grateful when I took off the saddle. In the light of a guttering candle I saw why. The saddle was U.S. Army issue but in very bad condition. Someone had made a hasty repair to the girth buckle and it had chafed a big raw spot on her belly. I also found a cluster of scabby wounds along her flanks where the man had dug in his spurs.

Right from there I hated Corporal Blewitt. I would hate anyone who could be so heartless to an animal that carried him everywhere without complaint and asked nothing more than to be treated decently. After cleaning and dressing all the raw spots, I began grooming the rest of the mare's mangy coat. Jupiter came over and showed his pity for the fellow creature by gently nuzzling her face and neck. When I was finished I gave them each a handful of ground-up cob corn.

It was starting to rain hard again as I headed across the yard in the dark. The stranger was at the wood pile gathering an armful of split hickory for the potbellied stove that kept his room warm. We ignored each other. When I got back to the house my mother was slumped over the kitchen table, her face cradled in her hands, sobbing. I put my arms around her shoulders.

"Don't worry," I said. "The war will be over soon and then Pa will be back. You'll see."

TWO

EARLY THE NEXT morning I was up to check the horses. It was another gloomy day, dark and rainy, with a harsh wind blowing up the valley from between the Massanutten and the Blue Ridge. I decided to let Jupiter rest in the warmth of his stall. At his age he no longer enjoyed the cold.

Jupiter was twenty-eight years old and stood eighteen hands tall. He was my best friend. In truth I guess he was my only friend. Black as ebony, he had white socks on his forelegs and a long white blaze down his nose.

My father bought him when he was a colt and had ridden him right up to the beginning of the war. As gentle as a heifer, Jupiter was also one of the fastest horses in the valley in his younger days. In 1849, the year I was born, he won the match race at the Rockingham County fair for the fourth year in a row with all two hundred pounds of my father on his back. When the war finally came, the decision was reluctantly made that Jupiter was just too old to fight. He still had plenty of go in him but tired easily.

After that we still had a lot of great adventures together, roaming the dark forest trails on the Massanutten, exploring around the newly discovered caverns near Weyer's Cave, and traveling northeast as far as Swift Run Gap to camp along the summit of the Blue Ridge.

As the war dragged on it became harder to keep him safe and well fed. Whenever the Yankees were swarming I would tether him far up Loft Mountain where they could never find him. I must confess that I also raided the cornfield at Lynwood more than once to make sure I had enough fodder to last him through the winters.

Now, with all the crops destroyed by the Yankees, it was almost a full-time job to find enough food to keep his weight steady. But even when I wasn't successful, he never complained. He would just stare at me, his big kind eyes like twin moons in the increasingly jagged face.

Going back outside, I couldn't see any sign of life from the stranger's room and no smoke was rising from his chimney. I wrapped my muffler close and headed off on foot for the village. An hour later I was lying in the window seat of Dr. Cassidy's front parlor and reading *Robinson Crusoe* in the pale light of the rain-filled sky. The words were alive on the page and I had completely escaped to that sunny desert island, far away from the sadness of my people.

"Hell's brimstone," thundered Dr. Cassidy, who was seated across the room in front of the fire. Hurling down the newspaper, he snatched up his cane and limped over to the walnut sideboard. I could see the blood filling his face as he poured himself another drink from the pitcher.

"Jeff Davis, that pigheaded fool. The whole Yankee army was flying like a flock of mudsills back up the Warrenton Pike toward Washington," he delivered. "I don't care what he claims now. I was there. God knows we could have driven them all the way to Baltimore and won the war. Oh, for an Epaminondas to lead us at that critical moment."

After four years of war, Dr. Cassidy remained convinced

that the Confederate Army could have finished off the Federals in their first great battle at Manassas.

"Remember the maxim of Napoleon, Jamie. No matter how great the confusion and exhaustion of a victorious army, the defeated one is always in a hundredfold worse condition. Manassas was our one great opportunity for a decisive victory and Jeff Davis ruined it."

Limping back across the room, he dropped heavily into his chair and proceeded to stare into the fire until his passion was aroused again.

"In the words of the great Augustus, 'Varus! Varus! Where are our legions now?' Thanks to those idiots in Richmond they lie slaughtered on a hundred fields. And today our remaining few are as Leonidas and the Spartans. Those poor noble boys." He finished his drink with two long swallows and put down the glass.

" 'Among the blind the one-armed man is king,' " he muttered.

"Eyed," I corrected him.

"I'd what?" he asked, confused.

"The one-eyed man."

"You're not making sense, Jamie," he said, shaking his head sadly. Knowing he was locked in the embrace of John Barleycorn, I turned back to *Robinson Crusoe*.

Dr. Cassidy was teaching me the classics. At least that's what he called what we were doing. What I was actually studying were those shelves of books in his library that Mrs. Cassidy had managed to save after the first visit from the Yankee army in the spring of 1862.

Dr. Cassidy was tutoring me as a favor to my father after they had closed the school in the village when the older boys went off to fight and most of the younger ones were sent for safekeeping to relatives who lived farther up the valley.

My mother was keen on the plan for another reason. During the hours Dr. Cassidy spent studying with me he didn't drink quite so much as he did the rest of the time. Not that I could see it was hurting him a lot. When he had too much to drink, his sad face would just settle into the cast of a dozing hound dog. Mostly, he slept.

That wasn't the way he used to be. I remember my father once saying he was the finest doctor between Lexington and Winchester. When the war started, he had become an army surgeon on the staff of his friend General Longstreet. He came back after Chickamauga with a bullet through his kneecap. Although he was not much past forty, his hair had turned completely white and his right hand shook like he had the palsy. By then, his oldest boy Harry was lying in a soldier's grave on the field at Malvern Hill. His other son Peyton had died of erysipelas after his leg was amputated following Brandy Station. After that, Mrs. Cassidy seemed to just dry up and get all wrinkly before she passed on in the spring of 1864.

I guess the tutoring idea worked out for both of us. It might sound strange to most boys but I've always loved to read. Maybe it's because both my parents were once schoolteachers. I don't know. But I started when I was five years old and have kept up with it ever since. Dr. Cassidy thought I should begin my classical studies with Homer and we had come a long way from the Greeks in the past year. Actually, there were very few books left on his shelves that I hadn't finished. And I wasn't about to read anything else by John Milton or Samuel Richardson. One was more than enough from them. The authors I liked best were Shakespeare and Cervantes. Among the modern writers there is no one I like better than Charlotte Brontë.

Around the time the stranger came we were reading Lamb's essays. My favorite was the one about the roast pig although I never thought in a hundred years that I would be feeling exactly like that pig so soon afterward.

On my way home I stopped at the Port Republic store to see

if we had any mail. Right then it was being run by Monk Shiflett, who was also the acting postmaster while Mr. Colston was
away at the war. What was odd about Monk was how much fat-
ter he kept getting when there was so little food to be had. He
was alone when I got there.

"That minister find your place last night?" he said while
pawing through the unsorted mail sack that had just arrived. A
new handwritten sign on the counter read, "No More Salt."

"What minister?" I responded, already on my guard against
his sorry sense of humor.

"The one needin' a bed. Looks like an Episcopal bishop and
ridin' a dun horse," he said solemnly. I wasn't about to rise to the
bait.

"He found us all right," I said. "And you're right. He is on
his way to Washington to preach to President Lincoln."

"Ain't you the funny one. No mail," he said, tossing the sack
under the counter.

I paused on my way out to see if the spectacles were still
there. A few months earlier I had accidentally broken the lenses
in my mother's glasses. It hurt to see her trying to read without
them. She had tried on the pair in the store and they were perfect for her. I would have done just about anything to get them
for her but the price was two hundred dollars.

"You better get on home quick," said Monk. "You don't
want your mama entertainin' that gennelman all by herself. I
'spect they all cozy together . . . readin' the Good Book as we
speak."

I made one more silent prayer to grow at least three inches
and gain twenty pounds so that I could punch Monk in his fat
dimwitted face. Of course, after doing that I would have had to
ride all the way to the store in Cross Keys to buy the few things
we needed. So I held my tongue and walked out into the dark
wet afternoon.

With the exception of Dr. Cassidy and a few others, we were pretty much outcasts in Port Republic. The reason was my mother. A lot of people didn't like her and I had read enough Shakespeare to understand that jealousy was part of it.

Not only was she the prettiest woman in our part of the valley, but she had the misfortune to be a Yankee from Corning, New York. My father met her at a teacher's conference they were having at Elmira College up around there.

Once I used to think it was the way she talked that also got people upset. Mrs. Paxton would say, "After all these yeahs down heah, when will you evah learn to speak propah." But it wasn't just the way she talked. It was what she talked about.

The thing that really bothered her was slavery. That caused some big rows between her and my father although he was against slavery too and called it the curse of the South. But he also thought the Yankees were two-faced since they had sold their slaves for good money before they decided it was evil and had become abolitionists. My father was no fire-eater but when the war came he, like General Lee, considered himself first and foremost a Virginian.

My mother didn't just argue with him, though. She wasn't afraid to tell everyone else what she thought too. People put up with it as long as my father was around. When he was elected to be one of the officers in the 10th Virginia, you would have thought we were the most popular family in Port Republic. But as soon as he left everything changed overnight.

Maybe it was because of my parents' divided loyalties, but at the beginning of the war I wasn't sure which side I wanted to win. I envied all the people who knew which side was right and that God was with them. Now, after four years of it, all I wanted was for my father to come home alive.

There was no sign of man or beast as I made my way across the river and headed north into the cold driving rain. It was over three miles from the village to the log house where we lived. My grandfather had built it on the side of the mountain overlooking the great plantation at Lynwood.

During the battle of Port Republic, the Yankees had put a whole battery of cannons up on the clearing below our house because it looked right down on the field where the two armies came together. General Jackson had to send a batch of boys up the slope to knock out those guns and they fought like crazy men all around our property. Finally, the Louisiana boys slit the throats of all the Yankee horses so they couldn't pull the cannons away. The ground got so soaked with blood that the stink lasted for weeks after they hauled the carcasses away.

By the time I got home, night had fallen. I was surprised to find the door locked. Rapping on the window, I expected my mother to answer the door right away. When she didn't I went around to the back door. It was locked too. I stood on my toes in the rain and tried to look through the kitchen window, but it was completely dark inside.

"Ma, it's me," I called out sharply. I knocked harder and shouted again. For a second I thought I saw a shadow fall across the far wall. Then I heard the lock being opened and my mother was standing in the door.

"Oh Jamie, I'm so glad you're home," she said, rushing to embrace me.

"What is it, ma?"

"Something has happened to Corporal Blewitt. About thirty minutes ago I heard what I first thought were the cries of someone in his death agony coming from the direction of his room. Next I heard the sound of a window smashing followed by more shouting. Jamie, it was truly dreadful . . . like someone demented."

I was gone before she could say another word. Slipping out the door, I circled the run-in shed until I could get a full view of his room above the fruit cellar.

A faint band of light trickled out from the closest window. Smoke rose in a curly wisp from the top of the chimney. There were no other sounds aside from the steady drumbeat of the rain as I moved through the trees to the rear of the little building.

Broken glass from the window lay all over the ground so I knew it had been shattered from inside. The jagged opening was still covered by a heavy gauze curtain and I reached in to slowly pull it aside. His room was a shambles. The oak chest of drawers was on its back and the spindle-back chair was broken in half. Stuffing material from the comforter was strewn across the floor. Of Corporal Blewitt there was no sign.

I went around to the door and let myself in. Someone had left the stove grate open and it was so hot in there I could barely breathe. That wasn't the worst of it. A foul smell filled the room as if something had crawled in from the bottom of a privy.

Then I saw the sole of his sprung boot sticking out from the other side of the bed. Slowly, I worked my way around until I could see him. He was on his side with his back to me. Evil-smelling vomit covered his clothes. I couldn't tell for sure if he was even breathing. Reaching down, I touched his leg.

He moaned and rolled over onto his belly.

"Who goes there?" he moaned.

"Jamie. Jamie Lockhart," I said.

Slowly, he clawed his way up the edge of the bed and onto his knees. In the dim glow from the stove the hairy face loomed up to mine, his wild eyes trying to focus on me.

"The runt," he finally said. Then he dropped back down and started crawling about the floor, sifting through the debris.

My guess was that he had acted out some horrible nightmare since there was no sign of anyone else having been there. As he rooted under the bed, he began mumbling incoherently about his "medsin." Finally, he emerged clutching the clay jug I had last seen hanging from his saddle. He greedily tipped it over his sucking lips but received no satisfaction. It was empty. With a groan he slumped to the floor again.

"I'm sick," he wailed piteously. "Real bad sick."

I now had a pretty good idea what kind of medicine he needed. The same kind that Dr. Cassidy was using.

Maybe there was a look of recognition in my face because the next thing the stranger said was, "Now you look a smart boy." A crafty smile suddenly played across his lips.

"You know where I cain get some corn?"

"Whiskey?"

"Not sippin' whiskey. Just nigger pot. Red-eye."

"I might."

"How much?"

"Fifty a quart."

"I ain't no fresh fish, sonny," he barked angrily.

"Suit yourself," I said, heading for the door.

"Now jest hold on a minute," he whined. After rubbing his filthy hands across his face several times, he said, "S'all right. You got yisself a deal."

"Who's going to pay for all this damage?" I said from my new position of strength. By the time I was finished, we had settled everything. I would supply him with a quart a day, cash before delivery.

I never stopped to wonder why he didn't want to go out to get it himself.

THREE

THOSE FIRST DAYS after the stranger came were very profitable. Every day after my lessons with Dr. Cassidy, I would go to his room and he would hand over another fifty dollars. Then I'd saddle Jupiter and we would ride north to the small farm outside McGaheysville where a farmer named Kydd would sell me a quart jar full of "gray mule." I don't know why it was called that since he said it was made from yams. It was the same elixir Dr. Cassidy sent me there to buy for him.

Mr. Kydd charged between ten and fifteen dollars Confederate for each quart of the stuff, depending on its "authority," so I was making at least thirty-five a day clear profit. On my way home I would calculate in my head the amount I still needed before I could buy the spectacles for my mother.

Gray mule definitely agreed with the stranger too. After I brought him his first jar he didn't suffer any more violent fits. To my knowledge, he never left his room at all except to use the privy and come to the house for his meals. I did ask him once why he never went to the village and he said the daylight hurt his eyes ever since an exploding shell had blown grit into them. I had no reason then not to take him at his word.

Most afternoons I took the old musket my grandfather had used in the first war for independence and headed up Loft Mountain to try to shoot a deer. I spent hours in the woods but never saw one. Game had gotten very scarce. Mostly it was because people were shooting just about anything that moved in order to have some meat to put in their pot. Usually I came home without firing a shot.

One night when the stranger was having his supper, something curious happened after my mother served him his potato soup.

"Ma'arm, 'tis a blessin' to body n' mind," he said.

Somehow I knew he wasn't talking about the soup. For one thing he hadn't even tasted it yet. He was just staring at her with a grin on his face as she was bending over to remove a pan of rolls from the stove. The man was queer. There was no doubt about it.

It was the next morning when all the excitement began. I had stopped at the store for our mail and found half the village crowded inside. It was impossible to get near the front counter and many people were shouting at the same time. For a moment I thought the war must be over and felt a secret thrill at the thought of it. But that wasn't it.

"Grave robbers, that's what I think," yelled Mr. Hannum, his voice hoarse with agitation. "Somebody around here's so desperate he'd steal from the dead. I've seen it coming too—ever since those idiots in Richmond passed that law keeping us—"

"Can't be," said Jack Rainey without letting him finish. "The graves that's all dug up are just beyond the hall . . . They's Confederate boys buried up there. Ain't nothin' on 'em to steal."

"Well, those graves are sure messed with. It's those ones from sixty-two."

"Could be hogs rooting," another man said.

"Three feet down?"

"The ground is turned over real strange," wheezed old Mrs. Miller. "Like it's been done from underneath."

Monk Shiflett said, "You think those boys are crawling out of their graves so's they kin go kill more bluebellies, Hannah?"

"There's a heap more chance of that happening than you taking up a rifle for the cause, Monk," declared Mr. Hannum.

"I'm goin' to kill all the bluebellies there is," cried Tommy Burke. He was nine and his father had gone missing two years earlier at Falling Waters. Tommy hadn't learned yet that no matter how many Yankees got shot there were always a hundred more to take their place.

I went over to the glass cabinet to make sure the spectacles were still there. I figured I'd be able to buy them if the stranger hung around for another three or four days.

"I don't know about ghouls or bodies coming out of the ground," said Mr. Sherrard, who owned Glengarry and was the richest man around. "I did see someone on the road before dawn this morning. When I started for him he began running toward the river."

Verne Sheedy, who was simpleminded, said, "I seen somethin' onct. Its eyes was on fire and it din't have no lips." Tripping over a sack of grain, he blundered into Monk.

"Keep your drool off me, Verne, or so help me . . ."

"You're all acting like superstitious idiots," said Mr. Sherrard. In a huff he turned and walked out the door.

"We've got to do something," shouted Mr. Hannum.

"Such as what, Carl?"

"Well, we could go up there tonight and wait for whoever it is who's doing it."

"That's a good plan. Why don't you do that?" said Monk.

"Somebody else want to come with me?" asked Mr. Hannum.

It got real quiet then and in those few seconds the answer suddenly came to me. That it was Corporal Blewitt who was the one disturbing the graves. I don't know how but I just knew it for a certainty. And that night I decided I would try to prove it.

I left the store and walked up to Fairfield Hall. The massive place had been deserted since the Fairfield family left for Lexington when the war started. Since then it had been used as a field hospital. There were graves in the fields all around the house. The remaining dead from the 1862 battle lay in a line near a low rock fence that bordered the overgrown garden.

There were fourteen in all. Most of them were still marked by small crosses made with hand-hewn pine boards. If there were ever any names written on the boards, they had faded out in the years since. With all the rain and snow we had had it was hard to tell exactly how many of the graves had been tampered with. To me it seemed like at least five or six.

I searched for a place where I could conceal myself if the need arose. The rock fence looked like the best possibility. About ten feet away from the graves, it was three feet high and made of uncut stones laid up dry. There was a shallow depression on the other side where I thought I could hide in the dark. After looking it all over I walked home.

That night I waited until Corporal Blewitt had finished his supper and gone back to his room. He had lingered at the table for an hour or more after the meal, trying to make small talk with my mother as she finished cleaning up. Mostly, it was about how lonely he was and how much he missed his own kiddies and the comforts of his good wife. Finally, he said he was tired and left the house.

Back in my room, I made some preparations for the night ahead. In addition to my long woolens I put on an extra pair of socks and my father's old heavy brogans. I carefully wrapped the stub of a tallow candle inside a piece of gum cloth and placed it in my coat pocket along with three homemade matches and a chunk of flint.

My mother went to her room a little after nine. I lay down

on my bed and waited impatiently for the mantel clock to strike the hour of ten. Before the last chime had sounded I was into my winter coat and slipping out the porch door to the little hiding place I had prepared among the straw bales that were stacked at the rear of the run-in shed. As I crawled in out of the wind, Jupiter called out a puzzled greeting. Then it was quiet.

Although I didn't own a watch, at least two more hours must have passed before the door of his room creaked open. There was no time to celebrate my successful discovery as his form moved past my hiding place and into the shed. A few seconds later he came out carrying what appeared to be a spade and pickax over each shoulder. Then he was gone.

Now that it was actually time to follow him, I suddenly found it hard to put one foot in front of the other. As I crept slowly down the path through the trees, a horrible stab of fear brought me up short. What I imagined was that he was waiting just ahead in the darkness and preparing to swing his pickax at me with all his might.

Right then I guess I would have been frightened of my own shadow if there had been enough light to see it, but when I thought it through I realized that the corporal probably had so much gray mule in him he had forgotten I was even alive. That possibility gave me comfort and after a few moments I was steady enough to go on.

There was no hope of actually following him in that black starless night but I felt sure I knew where he was going and so struck out for the village. After crossing the river, I skirted the roads and came up by way of the foundry toward the fields beyond Fairfield Hall. The wind ripped at my clothes and caused me to shiver uncontrollably.

There wasn't a light to be seen in all of Port Republic. At the beginning of the war it was a rare house that wasn't lit until late at night as a hopeful beacon for a departed loved one. Now it was as if by even showing a light people thought they were making themselves a more likely target for Yankee raiders or other desperate men.

When I reached what I could feel was the beginning of the rock wall, I ducked behind it and crawled slowly forward on my hands and knees. It took some time to work myself near to where I thought the line of graves began.

When I heard his voice I dropped flat to my stomach. Although I knew it had to be the corporal's, it yet sounded different, as if he had somehow gone mad from his strange quest.

"So where are you hiding, you black Irish bastard?" he sang out almost as a verse without a tune. "I'm comin' for ye, Lieutenant Shawnessy. Ye wake up down there."

For a long while I listened to the regular rhythm of the spade thudding against earth. Finally it stopped.

"So let's see who we got hidin' down here," said the corporal.

A moment later he began uttering a string of violent oaths and curses. Then like a demon possessed he began toiling again, the thud of the pick striking the frozen ground like a neverending drumbeat on the other side of the stone fence. I knew he was coming closer when he shifted to the spade again and the first frozen clumps of earth began raining down around me. The only time he stopped was when a dog began howling somewhere in the village and he waited to see if someone was coming. After a while he started talking crazy again.

"How is it down there in the nether regions, Lieutenant Shawnessy?" he called out. "Don't try to hide from me—not old Blewitt."

The corporal's voice now seemed to be coming from below the ground and I took the chance to peer over the edge of the rock wall. To my disappointment I still couldn't see anything through the blackness. Then the flying clods of dirt stopped falling. It was quiet again except for the whistle of the wind. I thought I heard the sound of cloth ripping and then a striking flint.

"Well, what do we have here?" I heard him say. And then, "Don't be shy now." There was a brief flare of light from what might have been a taper or an oil-soaked rag.

"You ain't as pretty as the last time we met, are ye now?" came his voice with a low chuckle.

"Give it up. Give it up. Give it here, you bastard," he said as if fighting something alive down there. Then all I could hear was the wind again.

He was breathing hard when he climbed out of the hole and began gathering up his tools. I knew he was coming closer because my nostrils were suddenly filled with the smell of the grave. His boot scraped the edge of the fence as he came over and then he was standing beside me, no more than a few inches away. A merciful providence kept him from tripping over me, and a moment later he was gone, walking fast toward the river.

As I sat up and rubbed the circulation back into my legs, my mind was racing with questions. Part of the answer might still lie in the hole, I finally decided. So taking the candle stub and matches out of my coat, I crawled over the fence and pointed myself in the direction of where I thought I had last seen the flickering light. I went slowly forward on my knees, feeling the ground ahead of me with one hand while holding the candle stub and matches in the other.

After I had gone at least ten feet I realized that somehow I must have missed my mark. At that point I lit two of my matches, but the fury of the wind killed their spark before I could begin to gain my bearings. I turned to my right and leaned forward to feel the ground ahead of me. To my horror there was nothing there. Too late, I pitched headlong into the grave.

The wind still whistled fiercely above me but where I now

was it had gotten strangely quiet. I was lying on my stomach with my left hand touching what felt like a wool blanket. Still woozy, I tried to pull it over me for warmth. Regrettably, it seemed to be attached to the ground.

Something alive began to wriggle across my face and I scrambled back up to my knees. It was at that point I discovered I was still holding the candle stub in my right hand. Striking my last match, I lit it.

Most of him was still lying under the surface of the earth. The first thing I saw was the gold braid on the sleeve of his uniform. The coat itself had been pulled clear from the dirt and the lining was ripped out. That's what I had first thought was a blanket.

Then I looked at his face. It might sound hard when I say that the actual sight of him caused me far less terror than when I had imagined the corporal's pickax hitting me in the heart. After the big battle in 1862, I had seen plenty of dead men. And every spring since, when the slaves at Lynwood and Lewiston began spring planting, they would plough up new bodies from the battlefield. The vultures would be waiting by the score in the trees along the river for that terrible harvest. Bodies were just something I had gotten used to. Not that this one wasn't a vision from Hell. I am not going to say what I saw slithering out of his nose and swarming over what remained of his face.

By the time I made my way home it was past four o'clock in the morning. Smoke was coming out of the corporal's chimney so he had obviously gotten back too. I was completely worn out. The idea of what to do about him would have to wait for the morrow. Dropping to my bed, I was quickly carried away in deepest slumber.

FOUR

WHEN I WOKE UP it was snowing again and I wondered whether it was also falling in the trenches around Richmond and Petersburg, where my father lay with the rest of Lee's army.

There were already a couple of inches on my windowsill and it was coming down hard enough to wipe out my view of everything but the run-in shed. It felt good to be burrowed in my warm quilts and I was falling back asleep when a muffled voice set in motion the event that changed our lives forever.

It was a man's voice but too low for me to hear the words. Then I heard my mother, hers loud and nervous.

"That will be enough, sir. I must ask you to leave."

I was out of bed in an instant. Going to the door, I cracked it open to hear Corporal Blewitt say, "You got to be mighty lonely with yer man away so long."

"Get out of my house," she said.

He was slowly backing her into the corner of the kitchen by the chimney. "You be nice to me'n I'll make it worth your while," he said as I stepped through the doorway.

"Keep away from her," was what I wanted to shout but it came out as more of a screech.

When he spun around, I saw that he had tried hard to pretty himself up. His hair was greased and the side parts were swept back along his head like a mallard duck. Somewhere he had found a clean shirt.

"I thought you was off larnin' yer lessons, boy," he said, obviously surprised to find me there. Then his whole manner began to change, like he had just arrived at Mr. Sherrard's bank to see about a loan.

"Miz Lockhart, I shorely didn't mean nothin' with them words."

"Corporal Blewitt, you will pack your things and leave my home," said my mother.

"It's jess that it's been so long since I seen my—"

"Now! This instant." She cut him off.

"My pa's coming home tomorrow," I declared.

He looked long and hard at my mother and then at me. "Well, if there ain't no room for me no more I guess I got to move on."

He headed to the back door and walked outside into the driving snow. I went over and locked the door behind him. A moment later my mother was in my arms and holding me like she would never let go.

"That man is nothing but trash and I knew it when I rented him the room. Forgive me, Jamie, for letting the almighty dollar overrule my better judgment."

"It's all right, Ma," I said, wondering whether to let her know what else he had been doing. I decided not to add to her worries. As soon as he left, I planned to ride to Dr. Cassidy's and tell him the whole story. He would know where to turn next.

An hour later there was still no sign of the corporal leaving. We couldn't see his room through the snow, but his poor horse was still standing in the run-in shed so he obviously hadn't gone anywhere. I finally convinced my mother to let me find out what he was waiting for.

The door of his room was open a crack and I swung it in far enough to look inside. He was just lying on his bed.

"You been holdin' out on me, runt," he said with a laugh. "Found this down in the fruit cellar and right good it is."

He was holding a tin dipper and pointing it down at a half-empty crock of hard cider that was sitting on the floor.

"Want a taste?"

I shook my head and said, "We need this room. I have to clean it now."

"So your pa's comin' home," he said with a low chuckle.

"That's right," I said.

"He an officer, ain't he?"

I nodded.

"A captain, I bet."

"Used to be."

"What then?"

"Lieutenant colonel," I said proudly.

"Well, the high an' the mighty," he said, scooping up another dipper of cider and finishing it in one swallow. Then he started laughing again. He laughed like he had just heard the funniest thing in the world. I waited for him to calm down.

"Your pa ain't never comin' home, runt," he said then.

"What do you mean?"

"He's daid. Didn't your mama tell you that?"

"He's not dead," I yelled back at him.

" 'Course he is," he went on. "Why, she told me so hesself."

It was all I could do not to strike his hairy face.

"You needin' a new papa now," he said, starting to laugh again. "Think I'll enlist meself."

That's when my anger caused me to blunder.

"I'll see you in prison first," I shouted. "You try anything with us and I'll tell this whole town what you did up at Fairfield Hall."

He right away stopped laughing. Then he sat up and slid his feet onto the floor in front of where I was standing. Maybe I should have tried to run but I wasn't going to back down to the likes of him.

His hand moved faster than a darting snake. In a second it had scrabbled up my chest and fastened itself around my throat. I tried to wrench free but his grip was too powerful. I grabbed the huge fist in both of mine and tried to pull it off but by then things were starting to go black. As in a fog I heard a voice shouting, "What do you know, you little bastard?", and then the world went dark.

I found myself back at the burial place. Somehow I was under the earth and two men were tilting a heavy gravestone slab into place far above me. Was this what death was? I wondered. Then I felt a cold wind on my face and I was back in the real world.

I don't know how long I was unconscious, but as my wits returned, I could still feel the pressure of his hand around my neck. It felt like there were needles inside my throat and it was hard to breathe. I was lying on the floor of his room and the door was wide open. An inch of snow had drifted over the transom and covered my shoes. My next thought was for my mother.

Standing up, I lunged through the door and out into the yard. The first thing I saw was Jupiter, completely covered with snow and standing saddled next to the porch railing. He called for me to untie him but I had no time to do it then.

Stepping inside the kitchen, I found it warm and peaceful. A pan of water bubbled silently on the stove. Aside from the wind whistling in the chimney, the only sound I could hear was the loud ticking of the clock on the mantelpiece. I looked around for something to fight the corporal with and picked up my mother's flatiron, which was lying on the edge of the stove.

I went through the parlor into the back hallway. There I spied something on the floor. It was one of her shoes. At the end of the hallway I could see that her bedroom door was not quite shut.

Moving silently forward, I craned my head around the corner of it and looked inside. Corporal Blewitt was kneeling on her bed as if in prayer, the upper part of his body resting on his elbows. I still couldn't see his face. While he seemed to be fully dressed, all I could see from across the room was the back of his huge greatcoat and the cavalry boots. For a moment I wondered whether he might be alone.

Then he said, "Do I got to hurt you agin? You keep playin' dead on me, woman, n' I'll stick you like a pig, I swear."

Knowing then what he was doing I gave him no quarter. He never saw me coming because all that hair covered his eyes like a black curtain. Although I still couldn't see any part of my mother, her other shoe lay upside down on the bed beside him.

Gripping the flat iron tightly in my right hand, I swung it as hard as I could in a wide sweeping arc. The edge of it landed with a sickening crunch on the side of his head. He collapsed without a sound. I dropped the iron and grabbed hold of his arm. Bracing my legs against the side rail, I hauled him off the bed. He fell with a great thud to the floor.

Released from his weight, my mother immediately rolled away from me to the other side of the bed and sat up. I saw that her hair was unpinned and the back of her dress was ripped completely to the waist.

"Is he dead?" she asked, her voice steady.

I kneeled down next to him and pulled the hair away from his face. The bones around his right temple were all caved in and there was blood coming from out of his eyes. I put my ear to his chest to see if he was still breathing.

"He's dead, all right," I said, standing up again.

"Good," she replied. Gathering the bedspread around her shoulders, she took some things from her closet and went out of the room. A few moments later, I heard her pouring water from the pan on the stove into a washbasin.

I couldn't stop staring at his body. As the sweet smell of his blood reached my nose, my legs began to shake so hard I had to sit down on the edge of the bed. In my mind's eye I relived the moment again and again. I had killed a man in cold blood without giving him a chance to defend himself. I had broken the most important commandment in the Bible. I was a murderer. Yet I felt no guilt at the deed. I found myself trying to pray for forgiveness but nothing came.

My mother called out to me from the kitchen. I found her sitting at the table in front of the fire. She had put on her other dress and one of my father's old flannel shirts. Her face was very pale and I noticed several raw scratches on her neck. She reached out and took my hand in hers.

"He told me Pa was dead," I said.

"He lied, Jamie. He lied about everything."

"Well, I killed him," I said.

"You saved our lives," she replied. A moment later I was in her arms.

Then she said, "Jamie, you know how people feel about me in the village, don't you?"

I knew.

"I'm not sure they would believe what happened here. Do you understand?" I told her I did.

"This will be our secret. We will never tell anyone about this—not even your father."

"I understand," I said.

The snow had turned to sleet by the time we had dragged him through the house and onto the porch. I went out to the run in-shed and came back with a length of manila rope. Tying one end around the pommel of Jupiter's saddle, I bound the dead man's legs with the other end. Then I went back to the shed and picked up the same grave-digging tools he had used the previous night.

As I led Jupiter down the track toward the woods, I looked back at him just once. The corporal's body was sliding easily on its back through the slush, his arms flapping out beside him as if he were trying to make a perfect snow angel. In the distance, my mother stood like a silent statue on the porch, watching until we dropped out of sight.

There was a boggy area about a quarter of a mile from our house where two gullies came together and that's the place where I buried him, along with the bag holding his hat, carbine, and a few spare clothes. The place was so thick with mountain laurel that the only way someone would ever find him would be if they knew where to look. After scraping away the top layer of snow and dead leaves, I dug until the pit was deep enough to drop him in. I was still inside the hole when I reached across his body to flip him over. That was when the low moan came from deep within his lungs.

I almost lost my nerve then at the thought I might be burying him alive. But with his head stove in, how was it possible? I was sorting this out when several things fell out of his coat pocket and one of them landed in my hand. It was a small gold coin. Suddenly, it struck me that whatever he had stolen from the lieutenant's body up at Fairfield Hall was probably still in his clothes. Now it was my turn to become a grave robber.

In the pockets of his greatcoat, I found a soiled handkerchief, a large bone-handled clasp knife, three stale biscuits, and a leather tobacco pouch. There was a roll of Confederate bills in his rawhide vest along with a cheap nickel-plated pocket watch. His pants yielded about a dozen cartridges for his carbine. I threw them in the hole, shoved the rest of his possessions in my coat pocket, and finished what I had to do. The rain was coming hard and by the time I covered him the place had become as muddy as a sinkhole.

Back at the house, my mother had removed every trace of his blood from the bedroom floor and also cleaned his room. Looking around, it was hard to believe he had ever stayed there.

I had one last job to do. Putting the corporal's saddle and bridle on his poor knobby horse, I walked her down to the river road and then rode north toward Swift Run Gap. Thankfully, I didn't meet anyone along the way.

When I reached the crossroad leading to Conrad's Store, I dismounted and tied the horse to a sapling at the edge of the road.

"Someone will be along soon," I assured her.

There were so many people desperate for a horse around then that I figured someone would be sure to steal her before daylight. I only hoped her next owner would treat her a lot more kindly than Corporal Blewitt.

When I got home my mother made me take a long bath in the hottest water I could stand. She was sure I would come down with something after having been out so long in the sleet and rain. Afterward, I told her the whole story about following the corporal to Fairfield Hall and what I had seen him do.

Together, we went through his possessions. It didn't take long. The only thing that seemed unusual was the tobacco pouch, and that was because neither of us had ever seen him smoke. I dumped out the tobacco on the kitchen table and carefully sifted through it. Aside from the fact it was dry and stale, tobacco is just what it appeared to be. It was only when my mother turned the pouch inside out to see if there might be something hidden in the lining that she found the map. Actually it was nothing more than a small piece of white bunting or sackcloth someone had carefully sewn into the bottom of the pouch.

There were a series of crude markings and diagrams covering its surface. In the state we were in, neither one of us could make the slightest sense of it and we finally gave up.

That night we slept in the same bed for the first time since I was a boy.

FIVE

A FEW DAYS LATER, two men from Richmond came looking for Corporal Blewitt. At least that's where they said they were from. I was at Dr. Cassidy's when they came to the house. According to my mother, the older one said they were hunting for him because he had deserted from his artillery unit. I had no doubts about that and a lot more besides. Yet it seemed strange that the army would send two men all the way from Richmond just to track down one deserter.

My mother and I had already agreed on what we would say if someone showed up looking for him. She told them he had packed his things and rode off three days earlier.

Where had he gone? they demanded to know. She said she had no idea. The two of them then spent an hour nosing around his room and the run-in shed before they finally left.

That was the same day I showed the map to Dr. Cassidy. Although I hated to lie to him about how I got it, that was the promise I had made to my mother. Things might have turned out a lot differently if I had told him the truth right from the beginning. We'll never know now. What I did say was that the map was inside a tobacco pouch I had found while exploring the battlefield. As I told him about it, he was in the process of carefully mixing several liquids in a laboratory beaker.

"My last spoon of sugar," he said wistfully as he added it to the concoction. Then he stirred it for a long time and took a sip.

"Ahh, the julep," he said. "Mars never received such nectar from the hands of Ganymede."

I unfolded the cloth bunting and laid it on his desk. He came over and stood by my side.

"Let's have a look at it," he said. Leaning down, he began to examine all the markings through the lens of a magnifying glass. They definitely captured his interest. He spent a good ten minutes eyeing it from every possible angle before rendering his verdict.

"Assuming this is authentic, which I am not prepared to do, it would appear that to the one who can decipher the code, this is the key to locating something of significant value."

"Why would you say that?" I asked.

"For one thing, they wouldn't have gone to the trouble of making a coded map unless it was important enough to warrant one. Also, the instructions are recorded in a way that preserves the secret from anyone who is not in possession of certain critical information."

He took up the magnifying lens and explored the map again intently.

"Another thing I can tell you is that whatever was hidden is probably located somewhere near Sudley Springs, not far from Manassas."

"How can you tell?"

"Look here," he said, pointing to the upper left-hand corner. "These are obviously the four points of the compass. Then there is the date, July twenty-second, 1861. That was the day after the battle of First Manassas. Now, I believe these lines represent the Warrenton Pike and just north of it the stream at Bull Run.

The marks to the west obviously suggest a dense wooded area and the cross inside the square is a church. Sudley Church, if memory serves. It is right at the edge of this line traversing southwest from what I believe is Sudley Springs. The rest is some sort of cipher. These things here."

There were numbers and words scrawled in ink around the borders of the cloth. Things like "200SE" and then "73W" and then "the Mouth of the Devil." Below that was a black half circle that looked something like the entrance to a train tunnel. At the bottom of the cloth was written "RBA" and then "Shawnessy." I recognized the name as the one used by Corporal Blewitt at the grave.

"What could the letters mean?" I asked.

"I believe I know the answer to that too. If I'm not mistaken it's a military unit designation. Rockbridge Artillery."

I remembered the corporal claimed to be in the artillery. Could he have been part of it?

"They were a unit of the original valley brigade. Ike Trumbo served in that battery until he was invalided out after Slaughter's Mountain."

"Mr. Trumbo who used to work for my father at the academy?"

"The same, although I believe he is now operating some sort of roadhouse near Harrisonburg." The doctor took another sip of his julep and said, "Ike is an honest man. He might be able to shed some light on the question."

When I had completed my study work for the day and returned my writing journal to the desk in the library, he brought up the issue once more. "You know, Jamie, if I'm right about the location being near Sudley Springs, then you may as well forget about searching for what was hidden there. That whole area is forty miles behind the Yankee lines."

By the following day my curiosity about the secret of the

map was whetted sharper than ever. The next step was to try to learn more from Ike Trumbo and I pestered my mother until she agreed that I could ride over to Harrisonburg to see him.

The following morning, she packed me a lunch of biscuits spread with corn syrup, along with a bag of sour pears for Jupiter. The *Almanac* was predicting another December gale and she made me take a second shirt and spare socks in case I got drenched. In addition, I took along a large piece of gum cloth with a hole cut for my head that I could wear over my winter coat if it got real bad. I wrapped it around the flintlock musket my grandfather had carried at Yorktown and tied it to the back of my saddle. It was a chore to load and prime but one of the balls would go through a good-sized post at twenty paces.

Jupiter was in high spirits at the chance for an outing and in the raw morning air clouds of steam billowed out of his nose with every breath. Although I also started the trip in high spirits, what I began to see along the road west out of Port Republic changed my mood very quickly.

It had been more than a year since I had gone to Harrisonburg and it was hard to believe what I was looking at now was the same valley I had grown up in. The great southern peak of the Massanutten was in the same place but everything else was different.

The first thing I noticed were the fences. They were all gone. Of course, there was no livestock left to be fenced in, but the road looked strange and bare without them. There had been so many different kinds. My favorites were the zigzag rail fencing made from hand-split cedarwood and the whitewashed triple-rail board fences around the horse and cattle farms. They had all disappeared, ripped down, I supposed, by both armies for cooking fires or to stay warm.

The only fences left now were the ones made from rocks. The soldiers didn't bother with those, although every so often I would come to a lonely grave alongside the road where a soldier had died and his friends had covered him with a cairn of stones.

Then I came to the Blackburn farm. I could well remember going by it at harvest time when the corn was taller than a man and lay yellow-gold in the sun as far as I could see. On summer nights, an army of fireflies would mass over its fields like a million tiny lanterns.

Now the entire corn crop lay destroyed in the fields along with their house, barns, and other buildings. All that was left of the home place were six massive chimneys and part of one side wall. We were told that when the Yankees came to burn everything they even refused to allow the Blackburn women to save their clothes and personal possessions.

The soldiers said it was because Captain Blackburn was an officer in Mosby's Rangers and had been guilty of hanging a captured Yankee over near Culpeper. Dr. Cassidy said the Yankee had been caught looting and deserved to be hanged. I don't know who was right but it was hard to see why it should have been taken out on women and children.

Many of the places I passed along the road seemed abandoned, gray and cold-looking, although at one farm a man was ploughing a rocky field behind a harnessed mule. It seemed pretty crazy to be doing that in December but the war had made people funny in different ways. I wondered whether things could ever be put back the way they used to be.

I stopped to eat my lunch near the place where Ashby was shot along the Port Republic Road. Someone had nailed a hand-painted wooden sign to the trunk of a big maple tree at the road's edge. It read,

HERE GENERAL TURNER ASHBY
THE GREATEST KNIGHT OF THE VALLEY
WAS MURDERED BY YANKEE COWARDS
JUNE 6, 1862

I once actually saw the general myself but it was only after he was dead. A few of his men had brought his body back to the Kempers' house in Port Republic and laid him out in the parlor so the people could pay their respects. The thing I remember most was that his blood had dripped through the seams of the crude wooden casket and forever stained the Kempers' rug. Otherwise he looked like he was sleeping although there was mud caked into his beard and both of his nostrils were filled with cherry blood clots. One of the women had put a red rose on his abdomen to cover the bullet hole.

Maybe it's because of my own size but I also remember thinking how awfully small he was to be such a big hero, although Monk Shiflett said later he wasn't a hero at all. He claimed the general went crazy after his younger brother Dick was killed at Romney. After that, Monk said, he was so reckless it was like he wanted to be killed.

After finishing my lunch, I started out again. Jupiter had just broken into an easy trot, like he was anxious to get to a warm place, when something odd occurred. From behind me a big hawk flew past no more than twenty feet above the ground. After following the road for a bit, it turned south across some wide empty fields. It was such a rare thing to see wildlife of any kind that I watched him go. When he reached the far tree line he soared high into the air and disappeared.

My eyes were still following the direction of his flight when they were drawn to something that stood out from the rest of the landscape. Since it was December, the trees were all bare of leaves and color. Even though it was too far off for me to be sure, I could have sworn I saw the outline of a horse and rider standing stock-still at the distant edge of the tree line. But that didn't make sense. There was no road over there. Nothing at all. I watched in vain for any kind of movement until we passed out of view.

On the northern end of Harrisonburg, I found Ike Trumbo's

tavern. It was a low flat-roofed log building set back from the road in a copse of white birch trees. There were only two windows, both very small, like they might have once been gun embrasures long ago during the first war for independence. Several horses were tied to the rail outside and an old man was sitting nearby on the porch. I gave him a dollar to keep his eyes on Jupiter and he seemed grateful to get it.

Inside, it was warm and smoky. There was a big blaze burning in the open fireplace, but it was some kind of trash wood and big cinders kept popping out of the hearth and landing on the packed earth floor.

Several men were standing alongside one another in front of a rough-cut wooden slab that ran waist-high along one length of the room. From behind it Ike Trumbo was serving drinks. One other man sat hunched over his own bottle at a small table near the fireplace. I made my way over to the end of the wooden counter in the far corner and Mr. Trumbo came over.

"Is that you, Jamie?" he asked with a look of concern on his good square-jawed face. I nodded yes.

He was wearing a hat with long flaps on it to cover the sunken cavity on the side of his skull but you could still see most of it anyway.

"What are you doing over this way?" he asked. "Your pa all right?"

I said yes, as far as we knew. Then I said, "Dr. Cassidy thought you might be able to help me with a map I found. It could have something to do with the Rockbridge Artillery."

"Sure," he said.

"It's kind of a secret."

"All right, Jamie."

With that I spread the cloth bunting out on the wooden slab in front of him. He looked at it for a few minutes, slowly turning it to read the words written along the edges, and occasionally shaking his head. The other men paid no attention.

The first thing he whispered was, "I think this might have been drawn by Lieutenant Shawnessy but for sure I wouldn't know why. But there's his name right there and he was the only Shawnessy in the outfit."

A smile came to his face as he said, "What a man he was, Jamie. Next to your father the best officer I ever knew." Then his face darkened. "He was killed at Port Republic, you know."

I nodded. "Can you tell me what any of this might mean?" I asked, pointing at the words and numbers.

" 'The Mouth of the Devil,' " he slowly read aloud and then shook his head.

"Was Lieutenant Shawnessy at the Manassas battle?" I said.

He nodded. "Our first real fight. Early in the afternoon one of their batteries blew a wheel right off our best gun. The men were all knocked down or in my case so scared I wasn't good for anything for a while. As God is my witness, Donegal Shawnessy lifted that gun carriage off the ground all by himself so another man could mount the spare wheel. Even after it was all over his battle fever was still up so high he took off with a bunch after dark to go bag more Yanks. 'Course by then it was all confused. No one knew what was going on. That was our first fight."

The front door creaked open on its leather hinges and everyone turned around. My first thought when I saw him was Jack and the Beanstalk. Pretty much everyone looked big to me but this man had to bend down to come through the door and once he was inside his slouch hat almost grazed the ceiling beams. He walked over to the bar and took off his gauntlets, laying them down on the wooden slab. Ike went over to find out what he wanted and then poured him a drink.

The men standing next to him resumed talking about the war.

"What about old Jube?" said one.

"He's long gone. Hightailed it way the hell south beyond Lexington someplace."

"Ain't no way he's comin' back now," said another. "Least-ways with any troops."

"They say Pat Cleburne may be coming up this way from Tennessee with a whole division . . . coming right through the back door to give that little Sheridan a boot in the ass."

"Would serve him right," agreed the first one.

"Cleburne's dead," said Ike Trumbo.

"Says who?"

Ike pointed to the man who was sitting by the table at the fire. "This officer is just up from Corinth and says Cleburne was killed with a whole passel of our generals in a battle down at Franklin, Tennessee. That right, Major?"

The officer looked slowly up from his bottle. He was clean-shaven and had a dark, bronze-colored face. His black hair was thick and straight and looked like it had been chopped off at the collar by a dull knife.

I had never seen anyone so dark-skinned wearing a Confederate uniform with a star on the collar. Right then, his hooded black eyes seemed very tired. The gray military cloak he was wearing had been mended so many times it resembled a patchwork quilt.

"Unfortunately true, yes," he said with an accent I'd never heard before.

When I looked back at the others I saw that the huge man was staring hard at the bunting which was still spread out in front of me. I carefully folded it up and put it in my coat pocket. He shifted his eyes to mine. Then Ike Trumbo came back, his body blocking out the huge man's face.

"We were talking about Manassas," he said with another smile. "Loved to see them Yankees run, I did. And we sure made them run a heap of times."

The next voice I heard was very deep and it came from beyond Ike's shoulders.

"Come here, boy." I knew who it was before Ike turned around to face him.

"He isn't doing anything, mister," said Ike to the huge man.

"You want another hole in your head you'll leave it well enough alone," he answered, continuing to stare at me. I saw there was something strange about his face. The skin was stretched real tight like he might have been scalded a long time back.

The other men who were standing alongside him began to back up.

"Come on, boy. You got what belongs to me. Bring it here."

Ike began to reach toward something on the shelf behind him, and the huge man slid open his coat, revealing a big Colt pistol stuck in the belt of his pants.

"Step away from there," he said and Ike did.

It was like my feet were glued to the floor. I just couldn't move. When he saw that, the huge man walked over to me. He was reaching down toward the pocket of my coat when the voice with the strange accent said, "Leave the boy alone."

The huge man stopped and looked around. Out of the corner of my eye I saw the Confederate officer rising to his feet at the table. My heart sank when I saw that his right sleeve was pinned to the side of his uniform. Upon seeing that, the huge man smiled.

"I didn't know the army had no nigger officers," he said.

"Je suis de la Bayou La Frenière, mon grand cochon."

"What the hell?"

"My parents, sir, were from the Attakapas . . . Acadians, if you will. That ancient noble race of which Longfellow sang in 'Evangeline.' "

"All the same to me. Keep out of this or I'll kill you where you stand."

"I don't believe it's possible for you to do that, my ignorant friend," said the officer, his piercing black eyes now afire. "But here is a proposition for you. If you leave now I will allow you to live. Otherwise you shall pay a small price for those poor manners . . . your life."

"That's brass comin' from a one-armed nigger," he said, and with amazing speed drew the pistol from his belt.

Almost in a blur, the officer's left hand flashed behind his head to the collar of his cloak and then arched forward again, grasping the tip of what looked like a small sword. I swear I heard it sing through the air before it buried itself to the hilt in the huge man's chest. His gun was still pointed at the floor when it exploded once and fell from his hand.

"Louisiana toothpick!" Ike Trumbo cried out.

The huge man stared down at his chest with what looked like a puzzled grin on his face. Then he started to sway, and slowly tipping over backward, crashed to the earthen floor like a felled tree.

SIX

IKE TRUMBO CAME OUT from behind the wooden slab and carefully approached the one-armed man.

"You ever fight with the Louisiana Tigers?" he asked, extending his left hand.

"Yes, I did," said the officer as he shook it firmly. "Major Alain de Monfort, formerly of Roberdeau Wheat's battalion."

I offered him my left hand too. "My name is Jamie Lockhart," I said as he took it. "Thank you."

He looked down at me closely and smiled. Then, moving over to the dying man, he planted a boot on his chest and began to drag the weapon out of his massive body like King Arthur removing the sword from the stone. When he was finished he wiped the blade on the man's sleeve.

"I hope it was worth your life, my large friend," he said.

The huge man neither complained nor uttered a sound. I only knew he was still alive because his eyes kept opening and shutting as tears flowed freely down his cheeks. Finally, his lips began to move but the words were too low for me to hear. I leant closer.

"Stonewall Jackson's gold," he murmured.

"What'd he say?" demanded one of the men. "I couldn't make it out."

"He said he's cold," said Major de Monfort, who was the only other person beside me close enough to hear him. Then the huge man's eyes went lifeless, he shivered and lay still.

At the same moment the door flew open again and the old man who had been watching the horses limped into the room.

"Riders comin' hard, Ike," he called out.

"Yankees?" asked Ike.

"Don't know yet."

We all stepped out onto the porch. Now I could hear the pounding hoofbeats of many horses coming up the Dayton road.

"No Yanks down that way," said Ike.

Major de Monfort leant down and whispered, "I would not be surprised if they were the friends of the gentleman who is lying inside on the floor," he said calmly. "I gather you have something of significant value to them."

I didn't say anything.

"You are welcome to ride with me," he said, mounting the large bay mare tethered farther down the rail.

Jupiter was tugging at his looped reins as if he also knew it was time to go. I untied him and climbed into the saddle. As I looked back down the Dayton road, I could now see the riders clearly. There were six of them, riding abreast and practically filling the highway.

With the slightest nudge from my heels, Jupiter leapt forward and broke into a full gallop. As the wind rushed past my face I saw that Major de Monfort's horse was keeping up with us almost stride for stride. Even with only one arm he rode with a smoothness and skill that made it seem as if he and his horse were one.

As we approached the outskirts of the city, the major reined up at the entrance yard to Monger's Lumber Mill. There was no sign of our pursuers and we could no longer hear them coming.

"They probably stopped to learn what they could at the tavern," he said, "but they will be coming soon. Do you know another route to the Valley Pike going north toward Winchester? One they might not know?"

"Follow me," I cried. With another nudge in the flanks, Jupiter sprang forward and we were off again. We rode east for about a mile and then turned north on the Keezletown road. Farther on we cut back across several open pastures until we reached the old forest trail that skirted the western base of the Massanutten. By late afternoon we were out of the forest and resting the horses in a small meadow along the ridge line. From there it was possible to look back almost a mile in the direction we had come.

Spreading out my gum cloth, I lay on my back in the grass. The whole sky was now one massive cloud of gunmetal-blue and it seemed to be coming right down on top of us.

"Have you ever seen a sky this color before?" I asked with concern. He shook his head.

"There is a tempest brewing up there and we will see it before long. The wind is coming up too," he said, staring to the north.

I closed my eyes and a moment later was asleep. I came awake to someone jostling my shoulder. The major said, "Wake up, Jamie. They are coming."

I sat up and looked down the ridge from where we had come. Sure enough, six riders were coming on in an easy trot, straight toward us, no more than a half mile away.

"How could they . . . ?" I began, but the major didn't wait for the rest of my words.

"One of them is a tracker," he said, mounting his horse and grabbing the reins in his left hand. "We have to fly."

It was a race for our lives. That was the long and short of it. Of course, Jupiter loved to race. He was already snorting in anticipation, eager to be on our way. Perhaps he was remembering all those winning match races. But at his age, how far could he run before he was played out? I couldn't ask for all his strength.

Heading straight down to the Valley Pike, we turned north, keeping the horses in a steady lope all the way to Lacey Spring. As we rode along I couldn't stop thinking about what had happened at the tavern. Over and over I saw the huge man falling and then, before he died, hearing him whisper, "Stonewall Jackson's gold."

Maybe it sounds crazy now but right then I decided I would try to find the gold and take it to General Lee. He would know how to use it to save the lives of his soldiers. I thought of how many winter coats and how many pairs of shoes it would buy for my father and the rest of his men in that scarecrow army before they froze to death. And there was one other thing. I knew I couldn't go home again without Corporal Blewitt's friends following me there to take back the map. Then I would be putting my mother in danger too.

That was my plan, but first I needed to convince Major de Monfort to go with me to Sudley Springs and find it.

"Did you hear what that man at Trumbo's really said before he died?" I asked the major.

"He said 'Stonewall Jackson's gold.' "

"That's right. Do you have any idea what he meant?"

"No, but I assume you're about to tell me," he answered.

"There is gold buried somewhere around Sudley Springs near Manassas," I began. Then I guess I lied to him, saying I had found the map in a tobacco pouch on the Port Republic battlefield and taken it first to Dr. Cassidy and then to Ike Trumbo. I concluded by asking him whether he would go with me to find the gold and then take it through the Yankee lines to General Lee.

"Well now, tell me this, Jamie," he said. "How did your friends back there find out about it?"

For a moment I considered whether to tell him everything.

Then I thought about my pledge to my mother. "I don't know," I said. In return he gave me a brief hard glance.

"I will think about the matter," he said.

The darkening sky had turned to night when the heavens finally released the incredible storm that followed. It began with the crashing boom of distant thunder and then a deluge of rain. I retrieved the gum cloth, poking my head through the hole in the center and tying it around me with a length of twine. I was soon soaked anyway.

Major de Monfort spurred his horse faster and without prompting from me Jupiter sped up to meet the challenge. We did not slow down for several miles. Suddenly, I felt Jupiter give out a great shudder and he began to quickly drop back.

"Keep that horse moving," demanded the major as he reined in his own animal. We were still on the Valley Turnpike and just approaching New Market.

"He can't keep going like this," I cried. "He's twenty-eight years old."

"You'll run him till he drops if you value your own life," he said.

"No I won't," I came back.

His face seemed to soften a little. "We will rest the horses for a few minutes," he said.

I took the chance to ask, "Will you go with me, sir? To Sudley Springs?"

He paused before he said, "Jamie, I regret that I cannot. There is something I am required to do in Winchester."

"But the Yankees hold Winchester," I protested.

"That is so," he said, adding nothing further about it. "You are welcome to ride with me but otherwise I must take leave of you."

"I'm going through the New Market Gap," I said with anger in my voice.

He looked down for a moment and a stream of rainwater

poured off the brim of his hat and soaked his patched cloak. Then he said, "That mountain pass is treacherous at night and I do not like the thought of a boy your age on the road alone with those men after you. But my orders give me no allowance to go with you. If you're determined to proceed with this idea, my suggestion would be for you to go through the gap as far as you can. Stay off the main road after daylight. This storm should be a help in disguising your tracks. Try to find a good place to hide, then wait until nightfall and proceed through the far pass across the Blue Ridge."

I nodded my understanding. As we were about to part, he edged his horse close to Jupiter and grasped my hand. "If you find yourself in trouble I want you to remember that on the other side of Massies Glen you will come to a settlement called Calvary. Ask for the house of a man named Gamage and tell him that Montague sent you there for help. He will assist you in every way possible."

Who is Montague? I wondered, but there was no time to think of any of it then. The sound of the rain pummeling my hat was making my ears ring.

"One last thing, Jamie. If those men do catch up and find that map on you, they will kill you. Do not doubt that for a moment. They will not take a chance on leaving you alive. Try to commit the map to memory and then destroy it. The knowledge will give you something to bargain with. Now move along and quickly. Your horse is almost played out."

He slapped Jupiter on the rump and we were off again.

"I can promise you a good head start," he called after me. Turning around in the saddle, I saw him slide what looked like a Sharps rifle out of his blanket roll. Then he disappeared into the wall of rain on the far side of the road.

It was hard for me to imagine how a one-armed man could even fire a Sharps rifle, much less hold off a gang of determined men with it. But I had seen what he did at the tavern and silently prayed that he wouldn't be hurt or killed in the fight.

In New Market, I rode up the pike until I reached the road junction that led east toward the high mountain pass. Looking for a place to get out of the rain, I pulled up under the extended roof of a seed supply warehouse. Still in the saddle, I lit the stub of my candle, removed the bunting from my coat, and once again studied the map that was already responsible for the murders of at least two men. After a minute, I laid it down. Closing my eyes, I tried to bring it all back in my mind. And there it was, as clear as could be. I held the edge of the bunting to the flame and it began to turn brown.

It was then I heard the first retort of gunfire. It was dulled by the pounding rain but after four years of fighting in the valley, I definitely knew the sound. It was quickly followed by the crack of more rifles.

Suddenly, the information on the map disappeared from my brain. As hard as I tried, I couldn't bring it back. What if I forgot one of the key points, I thought. Feeling the hot wax of the candle dripping onto my hand, I snuffed the flame before the cloth actually took fire. There would be time to memorize it later, I decided, folding the map into a small square and shoving it into the space between the pommel and Jupiter's saddle blanket. Then, we trotted out into the pouring rain and up toward the black mountain.

SEVEN

 It was like no other storm I had ever seen before. The ice rain hit me everywhere at once, making my eyes raw, pouring through the neck hole of the gum cloth and down my pants into my boots, filling them with water.

I had ridden up through the New Market Gap just once before and that was with my father on a beautiful summer day when the terrible cliffs were exciting to behold. Now I knew they were up there far above me, but cloaked from my sight by the wind and rain. Fortunately, Jupiter seemed to have regained his strength, and although the road was turned into a muddy sea, he forged through it with his strong, powerful gait.

It was about two miles from the town of New Market to the base of the mountain and I knew we had reached it when I felt the ground sheer upward as Jupiter started to climb the steep grade.

The road stayed pretty straight for another mile but after that it became full of twists and turns. An hour would go by and I would think we were making real progress toward reaching the summit. Then, in a flash of lightning, I would look back across a gorge to where we had been earlier, and it was no more than a stone's throw away.

The anger of the wind rose steadily as we climbed higher into the black night. It seemed to scream at me and tear at my clothing. Sometimes it came from all angles at once, like a whirlwind. I pulled my hat down low over my ears so it wouldn't blow off. Even so, I could now hear the roar of a cataclysm of water falling from somewhere high above us.

Once I thought I heard the howling cry of an animal or a person in distress. It was hard to tell because in that tempest every sound was carried away an instant later. Whatever it was, it didn't like its situation any more than I did mine.

The air was definitely getting colder and soon the rain turned to sleet, slashing at my face and finding its way through every tiny opening in my clothes. It hurt to breathe and my whole body ached from soreness and the cold.

Maybe it was the combination of riding thirty miles and the exhaustion of the chase, but in spite of everything I fell asleep as Jupiter kept gamely working his way toward the summit.

I was jolted awake by a roaring wall of noise, only to find we were no longer moving. Jupiter's head was drooped low to the ground, motionless, as if his great body were paralyzed. Ten feet ahead of us, the roadbed was completely gone, torn away from the wall of the cliff. In its place was a raging cataract of water that plunged down like a waterfall from far above and then disappeared over the edge of the track into the abyss below.

My first concern was Jupiter. Dismounting, I tried to lift his head in my arms but it hung there like dead weight. His eyes were half-open and unseeing. When I examined his legs I found he was bleeding badly from one of his fetlocks as well as the coronets on both rear feet where the horn met the skin. Considering what he had come through, that was no surprise. It was only when I put my ear to his breast that I became sick with fear. I could hear the congestion in his lungs as he labored to breathe. Even worse was the sound of his heart, which was beating fast and fluttery.

As hard as it is to admit it now, I began to shake. It started in my hands but soon seemed to take control of my whole body. There was nothing I could do about it. It wasn't the fear of what would happen if those men caught up to me. It was my terror of what I would have to do if Jupiter broke down here in this godforsaken place on the mountain.

Another few minutes must have passed and still he remained almost motionless. I knew that once he went down he would never get up again. Just the thought of having to shoot him set off another wave of shaking.

I was rescued by a book. It's true. I suddenly remembered a story I had read in Dr. Cassidy's library about Marshal Turenne, the great French soldier of the Bourbons. He was of a cowardly temperament like me, and his legs trembled so much on the eve of a battle that he found it hard to mount his horse. Looking down at his legs, he would say, "If you could foresee the danger into which I'm going to take you, you would tremble even more."

It was the knowledge that I wasn't alone in my disgrace that helped me to finally stop shaking and make a decision. There was really only one thing to be done and that was to get Jupiter off the mountain as soon as possible and find a place for us to lay up and rest.

I went forward to look more closely at the obstruction ahead of us. In the darkness it was impossible to know how far the river of water extended. However, I now saw that a narrow fragment of the roadbed had not been carried away. It was a jagged ledge next to the face of the cliff about four feet wide. There was no way to tell how far it extended, but if we hugged the wall, it might be possible to get across on it. At the same time it was possible that the force of the torrent would simply sweep us from the ledge and into the void below. There was no way to find out without going.

Jupiter was watching me as I returned. His eyes were focused again and he appeared a little more alert. I took up the reins and gently led him forward. A moment later we were inside the cataract and feeling the brute force of that mighty cascade.

We made it through because of something I never saw before we entered the black wall of water. There was a promontory above us on the face of the cliff wall that carried most of the water's power a few feet out and away from the ledge. This also explained why the ledge was still there. The whole ordeal lasted no more than ten seconds and then we were through to the other side.

My hat was gone but I counted myself lucky in the exchange, and continued leading Jupiter on foot until we finally reached the summit. Although the wind and sleet continued unabated, the going became much easier now as we began our descent down the other side. Climbing back into the saddle, I leaned forward and buried my face in his mane, keeping it there as he headed down toward the Luray Valley. Soon I was asleep once more.

I awoke to feel the gentle prodding of Jupiter's nose at my right knee. We were stopped on the road again, but this time I sensed the danger was over. The storm had ended and everything around me was covered in heavy mist. I knew that dawn would be breaking soon and remembered the major's warning to stay off the main road after daylight.

The landscape around us was densely forested. What looked like creepers connected by gigantic vines hung down in clumps from the surrounding trees. All the ground cover made it seem like a good place to lay up. Dismounting, I led Jupiter away from the road and along a fast-running brook to cover our tracks. Farther on, we cut through the thick undergrowth to go deeper into the forest. Eventually, we came to a small glade where several dead trees had recently fallen near another stream. Removing Jupiter's bridle and saddle, I first let him drink and then fed him all the sour pears in my satchel bag while I ate the last of my mother's biscuits. After treating his cuts with one of Dr. Cassidy's ointments, I left him to forage and rest.

In a soft mossy spot between the fallen trees, I rolled myself up in the gum cloth, pulling the top edge over my head until I couldn't see my breath anymore. As the wind whistled through the branches above me, I thought of my mother at home and hoped she wasn't too worried about me. A few seconds later, I was dead to the world.

It was well into morning when I stirred once more. I poked my head out to discover fog coming down through the trees around me like a woman's veil. It was perfect. No one could find anything in this muck. I fell back soundly asleep.

EIGHT

LIFE DOESN'T ALWAYS work out the way you plan. The next thing I felt was a hard kick to my ribs.

"Get up, you little sumbitch," said a raspy voice.

I stuck my head out of my lair to find that thick fog still covered the whole scene. The same voice said, "Where'd you hide it?"

Another kick brought me to my feet. How could they have found us? I wondered. The men moved toward me out of the fog like ghostly images. One of them was already going through my satchel bag and throwing my few possessions in every direction. He was a stocky man with big powerful arms.

"Figgered you'd found yeself a safe perch, din't ya?" he said.

"This cold is cutting right through me," said the next one, who wore a fringed buckskin coat and was old enough to be my grandfather. He had a lion's mane of white hair, and a long greasy beard.

"You mind if I build us a fire, Cole?"

The man he addressed was still hidden by the fog but I heard him say, "Might as well. We could be here a while."

The one searching my satchel bag had already torn it to pieces and thrown it on the ground.

"Ain'teer," he said. He then picked up my saddle as if it were no heavier than a man's purse and began to examine its seams. It was only then I felt a surge of fear as I remembered Major de Monfort's warning to destroy the map, lest they find it and then have no further use of me.

I risked a glance toward Jupiter's wet saddle blanket, which was lying on the ground just a few feet away. The folded square of bunting lay beside it, resembling a handkerchief more than a map, and partially hidden by one of my socks which had been hurled down during the search.

The one called Cole came swimming into focus through the fog. He was around six feet tall and my first impression was that he looked just like Ivanhoe, or how I imagined him to be after reading the book by Sir Walter Scott. He was about the same age my father was when the war started. His was a manly, unblemished face with a full head of shiny brown hair and wide-set black eyes.

"You must have thought you were well hidden, I'd venture," he said in a friendly way. He pointed to the old man in buck-skin, who had already managed to somehow start a fire with wet sticks.

"Nothing to be ashamed of. You were tracked by Claude Moomaw. During the Indian wars Claude scouted for Jim Bridger. He could have found you if you'd gone to Hades and back."

All in all Claude Moomaw didn't look like he could track his way out of the kitchen. A great lard belly splayed out from under his tunic as he leant over to stoke his fire.

Two more came up then. They both had red hair and looked like brothers. The older one was called Thurman and was around twenty-five or so.

He said to Cole, "Laddy and me waited like you told us, Captain. Ain't no troops on the road east toward Luray. Long as this fog holds, we kin go right on in."

"Fog's already lifting," said Claude Moomaw. "Be gone in less than an hour."

The old man's fire was now burning well. I only wished I was close enough to feel its warmth. The stocky man with the big muscles came over and stood next to it. He had found my grandfather's musket and smashed the barrel loose from the stock. Holding it up like a spyglass, he pointed it at the fire. Then he threw it away in disgust.

"It's got to be on him," he said. "Ain't in that blunderbuss or none of his things."

The captain stared at me and smiled. I had no idea what kind of captain he was but he had the kind of smile that made you want to smile right along with him.

"I'm Cole McQuade," he said.

I saw now that his eyes were not just black but had glints of gold in the irises that reflected almost yellow in the flames of the fire. Right then they looked like lion's eyes.

"I already know your name," he said. I returned his gaze for a few seconds and then looked down at the ground.

"How did you kill Blewitt?" he asked, as if discussing a fallen head of livestock. Again, I said nothing.

"Your mother is a very brave woman, Jamie. She refused to tell us anything. However, we found Shawnessy's tobacco pouch at your friend the doctor's. Unfortunately, he had no more to tell us either. Obviously, you were carrying the map when you left Port Republic. Since it may be hidden in your clothes I must ask you to take them off."

"If you've hurt my mother . . ." From behind me someone grabbed my right ear and began twisting it until I had to cry out. It was the stocky man again.

"Stop it, Dex," ordered the captain.

When he let go of me I took off my coat and handed it to him. He began tearing out the flannel lining.

"I just hope the kid was smart enough to keep the paper dry," he said, and the words sent a thrill through me. That meant none of them had ever seen the real map and that my mother and Dr. Cassidy hadn't described it to them either. All they seemed to know was that it was hidden in the tobacco pouch. Perhaps they had never even gone to my mother or Dr. Cassidy and were just trying to scare me. That thought gave me heart.

"You won't find it," I said. "I burned it last night on my way out of New Market."

"You did that and I'm gonna cut your heart out," said Dex, and I had no doubt he meant it.

The men were now searching through my things like they were hunting for lice. By then I was down to my long underwear. It was my only protection from the cold but I could see from the captain's eyes he meant to have it too.

As I stripped it off Claude Moomaw proclaimed in a mock preacher's voice, "As sayeth the man of Uz, naked I came into this world and naked must I leave it."

When I was down to my bare skin, Thurman began to laugh. "Scrawny little earwig, ain't he?"

His younger brother Laddy sniggered, "Why, a damned turkey vulture couldn't make a meal out of him." They were that kind of mean.

When the men realized the map was not in my clothes, they boiled over in anger.

"It's got to be somewheres," yelled Thurman.

"For sure I kin git it out of 'im," said Dex.

"Put your clothes back on," Captain McQuade said to me. And then to the others, "I'll have a talk with him later. Let's have something to eat."

That was when the last of the band came in from tending to their horses and I was shocked to see who it was. The man's name was Royal Bevinger and he was a farmer from Cross Keys.

Not only was he an educated man, but he was one of my father's good friends before the war. The last I knew he was serving with one of the valley regiments. Right now, there were lavender circles under his eyes and from the way he was coughing it was obvious he was sick.

"You all right?" asked the captain, and he nodded yes. "Stay by the fire until you dry out."

Mr. Bevinger came over and stood by the others but he wouldn't look me in the eye. Thurman and Laddy dragged several thick tree limbs into a rough circle around the fire and they all sat down. Claude had already driven crude spit supports into the ground and was expertly skinning the carcasses of several small animals he had shot during the course of their travels.

"How does roast squirrel sound for breakfast?" he wheezed.

"Ah'm so hungry ah could eat 'em all misself," said Thurman.

"Then learn to hunt," grumbled the old man.

I sat down and held my hands out toward the blessed warmth of the flames.

Right then was when we heard the sound of a gunshot from way back up on the mountain. It was quickly followed by a second. The captain was on his feet in an instant and heading for the horses. "Thurman, you come with me," he called out.

The red-haired man was put out. "I ain't had my brekfiss yet, Captain," he whined.

"Now!" came the response, and he quickly got up to follow him.

"I'll save ya the leavin's," said Claude with another wheezy laugh. A minute later we heard them ride off through the woods.

My first thought was that Major de Monfort had not gone to Winchester after all and was now on their trail. I leant over to Laddy and whispered, "Do you know what happened to the man I was riding with yesterday?"

"What do you think?" he said out loud. "We got around behind him and shot him daid." I looked at the others but no one said anything different. If he had told the truth, then I was on my own and would have to save myself.

Claude pierced the skinned animals with wooden stakes and slung them between the spit supports over the fire. The smell of the roasting meat was beginning to make me very hungry when Dex came around from the other side of the fire and sat down next to me on the log.

"Feels good, don't it?" he said. I nodded.

"Why don't you tell us what you did with the map," he said.

"I told you already. I don't have it anymore. I burned it last night."

"You burned it," he repeated, putting his arm around my back with a kindly hug. "Well, let's see about that."

Grabbing my left elbow in his powerful fist, he leaned me forward, propelling my arm out over the fire. My hand was now just inside the ring of burning logs and no more than a foot above the flames.

"Where is the map?" he repeated.

"I burned it like I told you," I said, trying to keep my voice steady as he forced my hand lower.

I didn't believe he would actually hurt me until the first sickening bolt of pain raced up my fingers and reached my brain. At the same time, Laddy got up and said, "I got ta go. Anybody still got newspaper?"

The rest of them were so intent on watching me they didn't pay him any mind. He was walking past Jupiter's saddle blanket when I saw him stop and bend down to pick up the white bunting from the ground. If he saw what was written on the cloth, I knew my life was probably over.

"Agghhh," I groaned helplessly, as the other men's eyes bored into mine. Over their shoulders I watched Laddy as he walked to a spot beyond the clearing, dropped his pants and squatted down.

Now the pain was terrible. My fingers felt as large as sausages and so tight they seemed ready to burst. Sweat ran down from my hair into my eyes. I kept trying to pull my arm free but it was like being trapped in a vise.

"Who knows?" said Claude. "He might taste a heap better than this old squirrel."

Then Royal Bevinger said, "Don't do this, Dex. The captain told us to wait."

"Shut your mouth, farmer, or you and I will have it out when I finish with the boy," he said. Turning back to me, he repeated, "Now where is the map?" I stared into his eyes in the hope I'd find pity there but they were like brown pools of glass.

"Burned . . . it."

I wasn't going to let them see me cry if I could help it. I tried to think of my father and everything he went through after he was shot for the first time at Sharpsburg. Never once had I heard him cry out through that whole painful ordeal.

Now Laddy was standing up again at the other end of the clearing and wiping his rear end with the bunting. At that moment I knew I was saved but at that moment I no longer cared. Not being able to hold back any longer, I screamed with all the power in my lungs.

"AAAAAGGGGHHH!"

As if in answer Jupiter began lunging high into the air at the place where he was tethered with the other horses. Desperately, I looked around the circle for one of them to help me. Thurman was grinning away like he was watching a circus freak. The old man was intent on his cooking. Mr. Bevinger's eyes were screwed tightly shut. I refused to look at my hand for fear of what I would see if I did.

I screamed long and loud again. And then again.

"For Christ's pity sake, put a lid on it, boy," Claude grumbled loudly. "I seen Comanche squaws roasted a lot worse'n you on the Green River with nary a peep."

I was out of my mind in pain when I yelled, "I KNOW WHERE IT IS. I KNOW WHERE THE GOLD IS!"

Dex seemed to take no notice and against his powerful grip I could do nothing. I looked at him again over my shoulder. The hint of a smile was frozen on his lips.

"SUDLEY SPRINGS!" I screamed. "IT'S AT SUDLEY SPRINGS."

Then, as if in a dream, I heard Captain McQuade yell from way off, "Let him go, Dex."

This will sound crazy but even though his grip never loosened, it seemed that somehow the pain was starting to go away by itself. Maybe I was beyond reason by then. The next thing I knew I was falling backward off the log. Dex was lying on the ground next to me and Captain McQuade was standing over both of us with the barrel of a revolver gripped in his right hand. Then I fainted dead away.

NINE

I CAME BACK INTO the world to find that Claude had slathered my fingers up with a greasy mess that smelled like herbs and rancid butter. He covered it with layers of moist leaves.

"I seen a lot worse, Cap," he said. "He'll jes lose most of the skin on three of 'em, is all."

Captain McQuade was down on one knee beside him. He handed me a small stone jug. "Drink this, son. It will help with the pain." I did as he asked.

Claude then covered the wrapping with one of my spare socks. "I'll need to change this dressin' tomorra," he said. "In a few days it'll be best to keep it open to t'arr."

I was given another swallow from the jug. It tasted nothing like gray mule but was a powerful spirit of some kind.

Captain McQuade then said, "We're staying here for the rest of the day. I want you to try to rest and then have something to eat. We'll talk after that."

He made me take one more drink from the jug and then covered me with a woolen blanket. Cradling my burned hand in the good one, I turned over on my side and fell into a fitful sleep.

When I woke again it was sometime in the afternoon and fiercely cold. I wondered whether Jupiter had been fed and got up to see. The others were all sleeping except for Dex, who was standing guard at the edge of the clearing, and the captain, who was sitting by the fire smoking a corncob pipe.

"You feeling better?" he said.

"I'd like to see about my horse."

He shook his head as if not quite believing what I said. Then he got up and smiled, saying, "You're a game one."

On the way to the horses, we passed close enough to Dex for me to see there was a knot the size of a goose egg on the side of his head. He turned away as we went by. Jupiter appeared content as he stood with the others in the tether line. One of the men had found forage somewhere and the horses were picking at the remains of what appeared to be dried timothy.

"I hope you know I wouldn't have let Dex burn you like that if I had been there," said the captain as I looked over my horse.

I didn't say anything. What did I care whether he would have or not? It had happened. That was the only important thing.

"I also want you to know that your mother is safe," he went on. "So is your friend the doctor. Neither one of them was hurt. Do you believe me?"

"What choice do I have?" I said.

"You'll have to take my word for it," he said.

"What about Major de Monfort?" I asked.

"Who is that?"

"The one-armed officer I was riding with."

"The man who killed Big Joe Braddock. A rather wily character, as you already know. As a matter of fact, he managed to elude us in the storm."

I wanted to believe everything he was telling me but there was no way to prove it. I decided my best strategy was to wait until I could learn more.

"Who fired those shots earlier?"

"I have no idea. Probably a hunter. We never saw a trace of anyone and came right back. That's the truth."

The captain's eyes had a mournful droop to them that made him seem so sincere. But then I imagined that others before me had probably thought he was feeling sad while he was beating them to death.

"I have only one question for you, Jamie, and you would be wise to tell me the truth. You memorized the map, didn't you?"

I paused for only a moment before I nodded. He seemed visibly relieved.

"Because you're the only one alive with that information," he said, "I'm going to tell you the story of how that map came to be. You may not credit what I'm about to tell you. There is no reason why you should, but it's true all the same. You know some of the story already. It all began on the night following our first great victory at Manassas. I was a young lieutenant in the 33rd Virginia Infantry then, serving under General Jackson. I was a good soldier. In that fight and for the three and a half years since."

He stopped as if waiting for me to congratulate him. When I didn't he went on again. "Well, that night after the victory we were celebrating what we thought was the end of the war. All of us figured the Yankees would give up now that they had seen the way Southern men could fight."

I remembered then a letter my father had sent home right after the Manassas battle in which he had written pretty much the same thing.

"That evening we were raising the devil in camp like most everyone else who wasn't wounded, when Donegal Shawnessy rode up on one of his artillery horses. He was with the Rockbridge but we had been friends at college before the war and were commissioned together at Winchester. He said if this was going to be the last fight then he was damn well going to meet some Yankees face-to-face rather than just watching them run from behind his Parrot gun a half mile away.

"I had seen plenty of Yankees up close that day but we were both full of Dutch courage by then and I agreed to go. He already had Blewitt with him, and as we were leaving my camp, Big Joe Braddock begged to come and I let him. You following this?"

I had knelt down to examine Jupiter's feet, which seemed better already. I stood up again and nodded.

"It was well after sunset when we headed up the Warrenton Turnpike after what was left of the Yankee army. By then everything was in turmoil. Our troops were scattered all over and no one was in control. The Yankees seemed to have dropped almost everything they were carrying as they ran. I'm not just talking about rifles and ammunition—I mean everything: wagons, caissons, tents, coats, you name it. We didn't know it then but the roads were blocked all the way back to Washington. Well, we were a mile or two beyond Centerville on a road that ran north off the turnpike when we overtook a Pittsburgh wagon that was stopped alongside the road. We would have passed it by but the next thing I knew we were taking fire, which sobered me up fast. Then we returned fire. It was over in less than a minute. There were three of them and two were killed outright. We found the gold when we searched the wagon. It was sitting there in three big crates."

He stopped to refill his pipe with tobacco. After waiting ten seconds I could no longer control my curiosity. "Why were they carrying gold in the middle of a battle?" I demanded. He could not contain a smile.

"They were Federal quartermasters. The gold in the crates came from two Virginia banks the Yankees had overrun as their army swept south from Washington. Those quartermasters were trying to get back when the panic started after the rout began. Then their own escort ran off too."

I could see it all in my imagination. The black night, the stranded wagon, and the frightened desk soldiers desperately trying to protect their stolen gold.

"So Donegal and I began to discuss what we should do next. You have to remember we all thought the war was over. I figured he was still behind the cork when he suddenly said, 'Why shouldn't we keep it? Hell, we're Stonewall's boys. We won the war.' At first it sounded so crazy I almost punched him. A few minutes later we were all agreed."

He laughed, as if reliving those moments again.

"So we turned the wagon around and started back toward Sudley Springs."

"What happened to the third one?"

"The third what?"

"The third quartermaster."

He paused for a bit and then said, "He was already badly wounded."

"You murdered him, didn't you?"

"We didn't murder anyone. It was war. They were the enemy. They tried to kill us. That's what war is about. Killing the enemy."

"You already said you thought the war was over."

He was quiet again. "That's true," he said finally, the mournful eyes looking straight into mine. "I'm not proud of it."

He must have seen the scorn in my eyes because then he

said, "Wasn't it Montaigne who wrote, 'Men did not invent devils. They merely looked within themselves.'"

I guess he might have had a point. "So what did you do next?" I asked.

"A mile back up the road we ran into a detachment of our own cavalry—Jeb Stuart's boys. In the dark they took us for Yanks and then all hell broke loose. Donegal took off in the wagon while the rest of us led them a merry chase in the other direction."

"And that's why you don't know where the gold is now."

"Here is what happened. After outrunning the cavalry in the dark, we doubled back to find Donegal but both he and the wagon had disappeared. We couldn't have been more than a quarter of a mile from where he was then, but there was no way to find him in the dark and we finally gave up and headed back to camp. Well, who did we find when we got there but Donegal, big as life. You see, he had already hidden the gold. When we got together in my tent he told us he had made up a map so we could find it again as soon as they let us out of the army."

"Why didn't Lieutenant Shawnessy show you the map right then?"

"What he did was hold up his tobacco pouch and say, 'Boys, it's right in here. And as long as I'm in the best of health it will stay right in this darlin' sack until we go back for those pretty boxes.'

"As soon as Donegal said it I realized that was the best idea. For one thing I trusted him and didn't really know the other two. Besides, we all thought we would be coming back in a few weeks to claim it.

"Well, it didn't turn out the way we thought," he went on. "The war didn't end there. That fall we went back with the Stonewall Brigade to the Shenandoah Valley to refit. And six months after that, Donegal was killed in the battle at Port Republic. He was in the ground before we could even pay our respects."

Maybe it was because my hand was starting to hurt very badly but I said then, "I know how important that must have been for you. I watched Corporal Blewitt paying his respects the night he dug up Lieutenant Shawnessy's body."

He shook his head. "I figured it must have been something like that. Is that when you killed him?"

"I killed him when I found him trying to rape my mother after he thought he had strangled me."

"I'm sorry, Jamie. I never should have sent him to Port Republic. Drink and defeat turned him bad like so many others."

Now that I knew the captain's version of the story I wasn't sure what to do next. Some of it had to be true. But which parts? And what was he leaving out?

"Where did these other men come from?" I asked.

"You're looking at a few of the remnants of my last command. Royal Bevinger was my color sergeant. The others happened to be the ones who were with Joe Braddock the night he got drunk a month ago and boasted he was going to be rich as soon as the war was over. You can figure out the rest. We had to cut them in or they threatened to reveal the secret."

He fixed me with his sad eyes again. "Jamie, I wouldn't ask you to make me a copy of that map any more than I would have asked Donegal. But I do want your word you'll not try to escape and that you will help us find the gold when we get to Sudley Springs. For that I promise you will receive an equal share of it along with those of us fortunate enough to survive."

Even then I knew that if anything happened to Captain McQuade, the only split I would receive from men like Dex and Claude would be a split skull. But my chances of staying alive were bound to the knowledge of what was written on that bunting.

I had to ask one more question. It went to the heart of the one thing that was important to me then.

"So you deserted your command in General Lee's army to go after the gold?"

"I resigned my commission."

"What about the others? They resigned too?"

This time he was silent for at least a minute. Then he said, "Jamie, I've watched a hundred good men die in this war. Men who gave their lives for a cause they believed in with all their heart. I believed in that cause. All the way from Manassas to Cold Harbor. I did my share. But that cause is finished now. It's dead as surely as Lee's army is dying right now across those mountains in Richmond."

"If I live I will take my share of the gold to General Lee," I said. "He'll use it to save his men."

His smile looked pained. "You're welcome to do that," he said. "My own plans are not quite as patriotic as yours, but the purpose I have in mind is just as important."

"What is that?" I asked.

I thought he was about to tell me but then his eyes shifted away and he said, "Let's leave that discussion for our next talk. What's it to be?"

"I give you my word I will not try to escape," I said.

As I lay back down near the campfire, I made the first of many attempts to bring the map back in my mind. It was no longer whole. Somehow it had become a jumble of unconnected fragments. Most of it was there but no amount of concentration could bring it back whole. I briefly considered going after the piece of bunting that Laddy had used in performing his ablutions but then rejected the idea.

TEN

THEY SPENT THE REST of that day talking endlessly about the safest way to reach Sudley Springs without running into Federal cavalry patrols.

Late in the afternoon, Captain McQuade sent Thurman and Laddy to spy out the road toward Luray. They came back an hour later to say it was clear, having also succeeded in stealing two saddlebags full of half-spoiled onions along the way.

Claude quickly set to work preparing a sort of onion stew flavored with the heads and bones of the animals they had eaten earlier. It turned out to be surprisingly good and I was grateful when Captain McQuade made sure I got all I wanted.

"Let's move out," he said after we finished the meal. Because of my hand, Laddy saddled Jupiter for me. When it was done I took a moment to listen once more to his heart and lungs. As far as I could tell he seemed to have recovered from his ordeal on the mountain.

When I was about to mount him, he craned his head around to look at me. There was an intensity in his eyes that I had never seen before. At first I imagined it was sympathy, as if he might have known how they had hurt me. But it wasn't sadness. It was a look of total trust, the feeling that we were in this together and would see it through, come what may.

As Claude doused the fire, he said, "One more night in the open, Cap, and I'm for it, I can tell you."

"You'll have your own suite in the Planter's Hotel when this is over," said McQuade. That set in motion a lot of big talk in which the others began spending their new fortunes. In their eyes I could see the greedy anticipation of pleasure that lay ahead of them once they got their hands on the gold. Captain McQuade never talked about his own plans.

It was gathering dusk as we moved out. When we reached the road, Claude rode out alone for about seventy-five yards, and then motioned for the rest of us to follow from where we were still hidden in the trees. Without any orders, Dex brought his horse alongside mine as we began riding east toward Luray. Royal Bevinger took up a position well behind us.

Soon Claude left the highway. The old man seemed to know exactly where he was going although I have no idea how. By this time full night was upon us again, although the first hint of a new moon provided the barest opportunity to see a short distance ahead.

In spite of my pledge to Captain McQuade, the thought of escaping was never far out of my mind and Dex seemed to sense it. He stayed beside me, never letting more than a few feet of space separate us as we moved through the darkness.

As far as I could tell, the rutted lanes and farm paths we followed ran roughly parallel to the Luray trunk road. McQuade did not appear to be in a great hurry and we walked the horses most of the way, stopping to water them twice as the long night wore on.

For most of the ride, Thurman and Laddy never stopped fighting. Although McQuade warned them not to raise their voices, they still found reason to quarrel about everything. Mostly, it involved the older one acting like a nursemaid and the younger one balking at it.

"You clean your rifle back there like I told you?" Thurman said at one point.

"Would you quit trying to be my ma?" Laddy answered.

"I'm your ma and pa and all you got, you dumb mooncalf. Mind me and you'll come out of this with your skin in one piece."

"I'll clean my rifle when I'm damn good and ready," said Laddy. Thirty seconds later they were arguing over which one was the better shot.

The new moon had long since disappeared and I was sagging in my saddle when the shadow of Claude loomed up on the road ahead of us.

"Good place to stop a little ways ahead," he said. "Another half hour till daylight."

"Where are we?" asked McQuade.

"I figure a few miles northwest of Luray."

We left the farm road there, passing the burned-out shell of a barn. Claude led us into the field behind it and then down a hilly pasture into a dense copse of sycamore trees that ran along a small brook.

"No fire," said McQuade as we dismounted.

I spent the next few minutes watering Jupiter and feeding him the last of the timothy from our previous camp. With my good hand I used a curry brush to give him a deep rubdown, making short circular strokes that penetrated his coat and caused him to shiver in pleasure. The familiar tangy smell of his coat made me think of home and I knew my mother must be frantic with worry. But there was nothing I could do about it aside from figuring out a way to get word to her I was all right.

Dex was still watching me as I rolled out my gum cloth and found a place near the captain to lie down. Wrapping it around me, I vainly attempted to find a comfortable position on the stone-hard ground. Soon, I felt rain spattering my face and bored deeper into my covering.

Sometime later I awoke with a pleasant sense of warmth combined with a weight that felt like a heavy quilt. Peeping out from under the cloth, I was amazed to discover several inches of snow covering me and more coming down every second. Raising myself up on my elbow, I looked around at the silent landscape. It was otherworldly. The peaceful mounds that were in truth the other men reminded me of sleeping angels under white shrouds in the most beautiful place in heaven.

I saw one of them stir and heard a monstrous sneeze. A moment later Claude sat up with a start, throwing off his blanket and its woolly covering from his shoulders. Then he proceeded to blow his nose into his hand. After carefully examining the contents, he wiped them off on the sleeve of his buckskin coat.

The others did not find the setting welcome either. Grumpily, they rose from the ground and began pestering McQuade to build a fire. It was obvious Royal Bevinger was getting even sicker as he wiped fever sweat away from his pasty forehead. The snow continued to come hard.

"We can't chance it till we get past Luray and all that Yankee cavalry," said the captain. From the foul looks he got from the others it was clear they did not want to stay where they were.

"All right," he said. "Although I don't like it, we'll ride today and then find someplace warm to hole up on the other side of

Blue Ridge Gap. With all this snow, the Yanks aren't likely to be about."

Before we left, Claude took the time to remove the crude poultice he had applied to my hand. Most of the skin was already sloughing off the last three fingers and they were very raw. Maybe it was the greasy balm he had coated them with but there was surprisingly little pain. He slathered more of it on from a flat tin of the mixture he carried in his saddlebag.

Thirty minutes later we were on our way. Claude took the lead again, far out in front. This time Captain McQuade brought up the rear. And just as he did the night before, Dex stayed close to my side.

Their luck ran out right away. A cavalry patrol spotted us before we had even covered a mile. My first inkling of what was happening came when I saw Claude whipping his horse back up the road and waving his right arm in a full circle. We turned our horses around and spurred them in the opposite direction as he sped past us at a full gallop. Soon we went by Captain Mc-Quade, who was now calmly sitting his horse in the middle of the road and balancing the stock of his repeating rifle on his right leg.

A little farther on, Claude leapt his horse across a low hedge and led us across an open field that stretched toward a distant smear of trees. I began to hear gunshots and swung around in the saddle to look back. At first I couldn't see anything through the increasingly heavy snow, but then McQuade's big chestnut came soaring over the hedge line in full stride as he raced to catch up with us.

That's when it happened. Even as I write these words, I cannot tell of it without a shudder of horror. One moment we were riding like the wind, Jupiter's powerful legs thundering on the frozen ground, with the other horses falling behind. And then I felt him suddenly stagger, his head plunging in distress. Pulling hard on the reins with my good hand, I brought him up short.

But before I could dismount, McQuade was by my side, grabbing the reins out of my hand and pulling them over Jupiter's head. As he savagely kicked his horse in the flanks I screamed, "No! You'll kill him!", but his face was set with grim determination and he never looked back.

Gunfire erupted behind us again and I glanced back to see a mass of blue riders, at least twenty or more, spread out in a rough line across the field. As more shots rang out, I prayed that one of the balls would strike McQuade and he would let loose the reins. But it was not to be.

Still we raced on, first one mile and then another until we actually began to gain ground, leaving the Yankees farther and farther behind.

And then it ended.

With one great convulsive shudder, Jupiter's great heart finally gave out. We were still in full stride when his front legs suddenly collapsed. Arms outflung, I flew over his neck and turned a somersault in the air, landing on my backside and skidding forward until I finally came to rest. On my feet in an instant, I ran back to him.

He was lying on his side, his powerful legs still flailing away as they tried to find purchase in the snow. I knew he was trying to stand up again and I wrapped my arms around his neck in an attempt to calm him. His massive chest was heaving mightily in a frantic effort to take in air.

Then I was lifted bodily from the ground and cast over the saddle of McQuade's horse. As I looked back, Jupiter was still trying to lift his head from the snow, his grieving eyes making a last mute appeal for my help. That was when the shot rang out from the captain's repeating rifle and he was gone forever.

ELEVEN

I HAD NEVER TRULY hated before that moment but now I knew the full meaning of the word. I hated Captain Mc-Quade for killing Jupiter. I hated Dex for burning me and I hated the others for standing around doing nothing while he did it. Just like that winter world around me, there was now ice around my heart. I wondered whether I would ever trust a stranger again.

Only the snow squall saved the gang from certain capture. With his uncanny sense of ground, Claude Moomaw led us through the white landscape in a wide slant until we had circled completely around the befuddled cavalry patrol.

The only thing I remember from that ride was McQuade trying to apologize for what had happened and telling me there was nothing else he could have done with Jupiter suffering as he was. I accused him of purposely running my horse to death. He said if he hadn't done it I would have been captured.

"You no longer have my word about not trying to escape," I said defiantly, but he didn't seem to take notice.

Two hours later we came out on the main trunk road a few miles beyond Luray. Captain McQuade lowered me to the ground and then told Laddy I would be riding behind him until another horse could be found. By then I was beyond caring what became of me. Sunk in despair, I also felt complete contempt for myself, knowing that it was I alone who had set in motion the events that led to Jupiter's death. Had I not gone after the gold, I knew he would still be alive.

Claude dismounted and began brushing a patch of snow off the surface of the macadamized highway. Taking off his cap, he placed his ear to the roadbed and motioned the rest to be silent for a moment. Standing up again, he said, "These parts will be crawling with Yankees anytime now, Cole. We've got to go to ground."

The murderer nodded in agreement. "Let's see if we can find a deserted house in back country," he said.

"That suits me," said Laddy, behind whom I was now sitting. He smelled of grease and sweat-soaked wool. Around the collar of his coat, his neck was inflamed with large red boils.

The snow turned back to rain as we rode east toward Blue Ridge Gap. We soon left the main road again, heading north for a few more miles until we came to a small farm lane that was different from any of the others I had seen in that part of the valley. The road was bedded with fine gravel and lined on both sides with rows of old evenly spaced elm trees. It ran in a northeasterly direction for almost a mile, finally ending at two high brick pillars.

I could now see it was the entrance to a large estate. A brass plate was imbedded in one of the pillars and engraved in capital letters was the name DANDRIDGE. There were no wagon tracks heading into the drive or any other sign of life. The gates were shut tight.

"I'll do the talking if anyone is there," said McQuade.

Thurman got down to open the gates. After we rode in, he shut them behind us. The entrance lane itself ran for another half mile, tracking slowly up toward the mansion, which stood on the brow of a knoll with a commanding view of the valley stretching all the way to the Massanutten in the west and the Blue Ridge to the east.

The three-story house was made of gray brick with a white colonnaded porch running all the way around it. As we walked the horses into the yard, I could see smoke curling from one of the eight chimneys that rose high above the slate roof.

Then I heard a door open and close. A tall man and a white dog came out onto the front porch. Although he walked with a slight limp, the man had an air of authority about him, just like my father, although he was much older, with carefully parted long silver hair and a distinguished face. He wore a well-cut navy blue suit. His beard and moustache were neatly trimmed and he did not appear to be armed. The dog looked like a cross between a wolf and a deer.

The captain spoke first. "My name is McQuade," he said in his politest manner. "We need fodder for our horses and food if you have any to sell. I'd also be greatly obliged if we could make temporary quarters for tonight in one of your farm buildings."

The courtly man smiled. It was clear his first instinct was to be hospitable. Then his gaze shifted away from McQuade and he calmly surveyed the rest of the group. The results of the inspection were revealed in his eyes.

"There is nothing for you here," he said icily. "You will have to look elsewhere."

I admired his coolness as he faced down the six heavily armed men. The dog took on a look of silent menace. He now seemed more like a wolfhound than a deer.

"I'd be obliged—" began McQuade again but the old man never let him finish.

"There is nothing for you here," he repeated with steel in his voice. "Please ride on."

Somehow, the dog must have sensed the danger because he bared his fangs and let out a low snarl.

"A man ain't braced got little to parley with," said Claude, grinning from his horse like a mangy likeness of old Saint Nicholas.

"I regret to do this but I have no other choice but to requisition what we need," said McQuade.

"By whose authority?" demanded the man on the porch.

"Too damn cold for this," said Claude, pulling his dragoon pistol out from under his coat and pointing it at him. "Here's arr thority."

A second later I heard the sound of glass breaking and the barrel of a rifle came plunging through a jagged opening in one of the large downstairs windows. After that it all happened so fast.

"Don't fire," yelled McQuade to the others, but he was already too late.

Claude's pistol exploded first. The courtly man's distinguished face erupted in blood and he pitched backward over the side railing into a large rhododendron bush.

The horses were already bellowing when I heard the next explosion, even louder than the first. Laddy flew out of the saddle just in front of me and landed headfirst on the ground.

Then, almost too fast to see, I saw the dog launch itself from the porch. In two bounds it was at Dex's side, and with another leap had sunk its jaws into his right thigh.

Screaming in pain, he pounded the dog's head with the butt of his revolver, but it still hung there, giving no quarter until Dex finally placed the barrel in his ear and pulled the trigger.

As Laddy's horse reared up, I fell off his haunches, scrambling when I hit the ground to avoid his thrashing hooves.

Then, the men were off their mounts and rushing toward the house. All except Royal and Claude. While Royal rounded up the horses Claude busied himself dragging the old man out of the rhododendron bush. As soon as he had him clear, he began rifling his pockets.

I crawled over to Laddy. The bullet had taken him in one side and gone straight out the other, leaving a gaping wound that was pouring his life's blood out onto the muddy ground. He lay on his back, his arms thrown out to either side, and staring up at the rain that still fell from the leaden sky. At first I thought he was dead, but then his lips began to slowly form words.

"I am kilt," he said softly.

His eyes turned ever so slightly in my direction and took me in. A little smile creased his thin, pale face.

"Now I lay me . . ." he whispered between quick panting breaths, "down to sleep."

"I pray . . ." he gasped out, but then his eyes turned questioning as if he couldn't remember any more words, and he died.

Claude had pulled off the old man's boots and was trying them on when I began to hear shouting from the house. Stepping up onto the porch, I went through the wide-open front door. A grand hallway ran all the way from the front of the house to the back. It was furnished with marble-topped walnut furniture and there were oil paintings of people from the revolutionary time on the wall next to the curved staircase. I passed Dex on his way upstairs with a drawn pistol.

The shouting seemed to be coming from one of the side halls and I followed the noise. They were in the library, although like Dr. Cassidy's, most of the shelves were bare. Either the Yankees had already been there or the books had been hidden somewhere for better times.

In the middle of the library stood an enormous evergreen tree, its tangy fresh-cut smell a sudden reminder that Christmas was coming. They must have been decorating it when we came. It was adorned with red and gold ribbons along with dozens of hand-painted glass and ceramic ornaments. A long string of bright red holly berries had been wound once around the lower branches of the tree but most of it still lay coiled on the carpet.

The windows of the wood-paneled room faced onto the front porch and several of the panes were shattered. A rifle lay on the floor by the nearest window. Right next to it was another body. He was a little Negro man with tightly curled white hair and wearing an old-fashioned suit. A thick stream of his blood was spreading out from underneath him across the wide-planked polished floor.

Captain McQuade had Thurman backed up against the wall and his hands were at the younger man's throat. "The man's arms were raised," he shouted. "He had given up, damn your eyes."

"He shot Laddy," screamed back Thurman. "He shot my brother!"

The only other person in the room was a slim woman in a green silk dress. She had long auburn hair, but I couldn't see her face because it was covered by both of her hands, as if she were trying to blot out what she had just witnessed. She stood slumped next to one of the big leather armchairs without making a sound. Then her hands dropped to her sides as if they were too heavy to hold up any longer.

When McQuade finally swung from Thurman to face her, she said, "Please take me to my father." The words came out so slowly I wondered if she was feebleminded.

As she passed me on her way to the door, I could see she wasn't much older than me, but her green eyes were fixed and lifeless. Even the way she walked was strange for someone so young, like an elderly lady with rheumatism.

Royal Bevinger had dragged her father in from out of the rain and laid him out on his back in the front hall. For some reason he had left Laddy in the yard. The girl walked toward the corpse in halting steps, waiting until she was directly above him to look down. Unlike in life, there was nothing distinguished about him now. All the pockets of his mud-drenched suit had been yanked out and he was completely barefoot. His face was a horrible bloody mask.

I heard her sharp intake of breath and a stifled cry before she slumped to her knees beside him. Standing next to her, Captain McQuade seemed almost transfixed as he stared down at them both, his mournful eyes giving off a weird light.

Thurman came into the hall crying, "Where's Laddy?" Mr. Bevinger pointed toward the door and he went out. He was back a minute later, having wrestled his brother into an upright position and then waltzed him across the yard and up the porch steps all by himself. Bringing the streaming body inside, he laid him down on the other side of the hall from Mr. Dandridge and burst into tears. Then he began rocking back and forth, sobbing, "What's Ma gonna say?"

The scene must have struck a powerful chord with Claude because it was the only time I ever heard him say anything good about someone. "He was a right boy, that one," he said, as Thurman petted his brother's face and kissed his cheek.

Still kneeling next to her father with her back turned to the rest of us, the girl formed her hands into claws that became like eagle's talons as Thurman carried on. Then she slowly relaxed them again. Pulling a white silk handkerchief from her sleeve, she leant down and gently covered his ruined face with it. Next she took his hand in hers and held it to her cheek, finally laying it down at his side again before standing up. Turning about, she looked at each of us long and hard as if memorizing our faces.

Her big eyes were no longer lifeless. They flashed like green fire. And then, as if none of her father's killers were watching her every move, she slowly walked up the curving staircase and disappeared down the hall. I heard the sound of a door shutting and then it was still.

TWELVE

NO YANKEE PATROLS came near us during the remainder of that day, which continued stormy. Inside, the house was bitterly cold. The wind took up again and it moaned down the chimneys and rattled the windows. There wasn't enough seasoned firewood to heat more than a few of the rooms, and as the afternoon turned dark I could see my breath in the light from the candle in the parlor where I sat waiting while the killers decided what to do next.

With the weather so bad, none of them were excited at the thought of digging three more graves. They did remove the bodies to the carriage shed in a small farm cart, and then made a careful search of the house. There was no one else to be found, although I did notice a table in the parlor with several framed daguerreotypes on it. They showed Miss Dandridge with her mother and what I guessed were two brothers. Of what had become of them, I had no idea.

The search produced meager results in the way of food. There was no livestock in the outbuildings and no cured meat of any kind in the house. Aside from several bushel baskets of apples and potatoes, the only provisions they uncovered were a few sacks of milled corn flour and a ten-gallon crock of cucumber pickles. The men were not pleased.

"If this is the way yer highborn folks are livin' I'll take the army," grumbled Claude. "Leastways we had our fat pork."

The one thing that did make them happy was when Dex came out from the pantry with a small keg under his arm.

"Lest I'm mistaken," he said, "this is Irish."

Apparently, it was a powerful whiskey because they began tapping it hard as soon as the stopper was out of the bunghole. McQuade was the worst, taking it down in great gulps and then going right back for more. By nightfall, he was already sloppy drunk. With the exception of Royal Bevinger, the others weren't far behind. He was sicker than ever at that point and just sat shivering in his chair with a blanket wrapped around his shoulders.

After a while, they no longer even bothered to go down the hall to fetch wood for the fire. Thurman started it first. After complaining about how cold it was, he went over and picked up an inlaid mahogany gaming table and smashed it to pieces against the wall. Then he fed it to the fire. Whenever the blaze died down after that, someone would just break up another piece of furniture.

By evening, they had consumed the whole crock of pickles and much of their keg of "Irish." That was when Captain McQuade tried to get up from his chair, stumbled, and fell facedown on the floor. He didn't get up.

Thurman was staring at one of the paintings on the wall.

"I bet they had thesselves some fancy balls in this house," he said. "We ought to have that sweet belle up theah put on her gown and finery'n come down heah to dance with us."

"Dammit's a fine idea," sang out Dex. He lurched over to the captain, who still lay insensible on the floor.

"What you say, Cap? Kin we have us a ball?" He kicked him hard in the ribs but McQuade only mumbled something into the carpet.

"Cap says fine idea too," said Dex. "You go on up'n give an invite to the lady."

I could hear Thurman bounding up the stairs two at a time and then he was knocking on her door. The knocking got louder until finally he lost patience and just battered it open. A minute later he was back with her. The girl was on her feet but being dragged along by her thick auburn hair. She was still wearing the same green silk dress that so closely matched her eyes.

"Lady tole me her dance card was full," he said, grinning like a simpleton. "Ah unfilled it for huh."

"I aim to fill me somethin' this night," said Claude Moomaw. He then sat down at what looked like a little black desk but which turned out to be some kind of piano that sounded like a harp. In the event, he had no idea how to play it and the musical sounds were harsh and unpleasant.

"May ah have this dance?" asked Thurman with a deep mocking bow. He tried to grab her hand, but the girl slapped it away.

"Lawd's truth," he said, "You ah the prittest girl I evah seen."

"Git on an put a bloom in er cheeks," said Claude.

Thurman took hold of her and she began twisting madly back and forth in his arms. "Someone give a hand," he called out, trying to hold her in place long enough to kiss her. Dex moved to pin her arms behind her back and she began to make little whimpering noises as Thurman had his way with her.

When I heard the sound of her dress tearing I didn't stop to think about what to do next. Being small has its advantages sometimes. I was able to get close up next to Thurman before I stamped my boot heel down on the side of his shin.

Right away, he stopped what he was doing long enough to cuff me in the head with the back of his hand. It sent me flying across the room but I was up again in a moment and on my way back to him when Dex dropped her arms and came forward to meet me.

Now free, the girl raked her fingernails across Thurman's face and three tiny rivulets of blood spurted up in their path. As she stepped back, I could see the white straps of her shift where the dress had been ripped away from her shoulder. Then Dex was on top of me.

The deafening explosion stopped everyone in their tracks. I looked up to see Royal Bevinger holding a smoking pistol that was pointed at the floor. He was still in his chair and covered by the blanket. As I look back on it now, he may not have had the strength to stand up at that point.

"No more," he said quietly.

"You better stay outta this, farmer," said Dex, his face beet-red. "I mean what I say."

"It wouldn't take much for me to kill you, Dex," said Mr. Bevinger in a deadly serious voice. "I've killed a lot better than you in this war."

Dex did not have his gun. Neither did Thurman. I knew that Claude always carried his dragoon pistol in a shoulder holster inside his buckskin coat. That was where his hand was going.

"Watch out," I called to Mr. Bevinger. The sick man trained his pistol on Claude and motioned for him to give it over.

"You makin' a big mistake, Royal," said the old man. "This ain't fogivable."

"We will see," he said as Claude tossed the pistol to him.

Mr. Bevinger turned and gave me a wan smile. "Jamie, you take Miss Dandridge and lock yourselves in the cellar. Give me your word you will do that and not try to escape."

"I give you my word."

"All right," he said. "I'll hold the fort here until the captain comes around. Then we will be down to get you. Go now."

I had no idea how long we might have to wait down there. Captain McQuade had not moved a muscle when the gun went off. But the cellar seemed a lot safer place to be right then. The girl took a pewter candleholder from the mantel and I followed her down the hall. Hard rain was pelting the windows along the way.

Upon seeing the strength of the cellar door, I concluded that Mr. Bevinger may have already known that the girl and I would need a safe sanctuary before that night passed. It was almost two inches thick, and the frame was equally stout.

I went down first. She followed with the lit candle and locked the door behind us. As I descended into the darkness I could still hear the angry voices of the men coming from the parlor and hoped that Mr. Bevinger would have sufficient strength to hold them off.

It could not have been below the freezing mark down there because I could hear rainwater flowing into an underground tank. However, the brick walls felt ice-cold. We slowly made our way forward into the cavernous cellar. In the faint light of her candle, I could see the vague features of the massive hearth that must have served as their summer kitchen. The girl led me to a small room beyond it where there was a trestle table and two ladder-back chairs. Sitting down, she placed the candleholder between us and said, "My name is Katharine Dandridge. I'm called Kate by my family."

It right away struck me that the men upstairs had just murdered the man who might have started calling her that when she was a little girl.

"My name is Jamie Lockhart," I said.

"Why are you with them?" she asked next.

"They took me," I said, and she nodded as if I didn't have to explain any further.

By and by she told me she was eighteen years old and one of three children. Her two older brothers were serving in the army and as far as she knew they were both still alive. I was glad for that because she said her mother had died of a raging fever the previous spring. But for her brothers she would have been completely alone in the world.

"How old are you?" she asked at one point, her face no more than six inches from mine.

"Fifteen," I said and braced myself for the words that I knew were coming about my size.

Instead, she said, "You are brave and true, Jamie Lockhart. I thank you for saving my life."

From that moment on I would have done anything for her.

"I'm sorry about your father," I said, "and your slave."

"You mean Franklin. He wasn't our slave. My father owned no slaves. Franklin was a freeman."

Her eyes began to flash green fire again in the candlelight. "If I have to search for them the rest of my life," she said, "I will see those men dead for what they have done."

I wasn't sure how long either one of us would be alive to carry out the search because the voices in the parlor had been growing ever louder.

"What happened to your hand?" she asked then, looking down at the sock that still covered Claude's dressing.

"The one called Dex burned me," I said.

"Let me see it," she said, and I brought my hand up onto the table. Tenderly, she began to pull the sock off.

"Why did he do this?" she started to ask, but before I could answer we heard a shout followed by a loud crashing noise. Then the floor beams above our heads began to vibrate as heavy footfalls pounded down the hall and someone threw the full weight of his body against the cellar door. It didn't give way, but another assault quickly followed the first.

I completely forgot my pledge to Mr. Bevinger when Kate raised the candle from the table and took my good hand in hers. As swiftly as a cat, she led us farther into the dark reaches of the vast cellar.

We were too far below ground for there to be any windows, but she clearly knew where she was heading. It turned out to be the brick wall at the farthest end of the cellar. As far as I could see we were trapped.

"Can you swim?" she asked, which at that moment sounded like a very stupid question.

"Yes," I said, trusting her to have some purpose in mind.

"Follow me," she said, and lifting her skirts above her knees, she climbed onto an old farm table that stood against the wall. Behind us, I heard the cellar door splinter with a loud crack and knew they were coming.

Now that we were both standing on the table, I could see there was a narrow space between the top rim of this brick wall and the ceiling beam above us.

"Climb over," Kate whispered. With that she blew the candle out and everything went dark. I felt her scrambling over the edge and I followed a second later. Holding my bandaged hand to my chest, I tumbled headfirst into a lake of black water.

THIRTEEN

WE WERE IN THE underground cistern that had been constructed beneath the house. It was a massive cement-lined tank that collected rainwater from the roof through a slue of drainpipes, and provided the house with its own supply of fresh water. I actually heard the rushing streams when we first descended into the cellar but had not recognized what they were.

Kate seemed to know exactly where she was going and gently pulled me along. I'm sure the water was cold but under the circumstances I don't even remember it. As we silently swam away from the glow of the searchers' lamps, the light beams began to cast monstrous shadows ahead of us. When we reached the far end of the cistern I came up hard against the rim of its outer wall and grabbed the edge with my good hand. Above the bricks ran a mortared stone foundation. In the middle of it there was a four-foot-wide slatted panel. When Kate slid open its locking bolt, the hinged panel swung toward us and a fierce blast of wind blew past into the cellar.

"What's that?" I heard Dex cry out as the lights flickered behind us.

"Arr comin' from outside," yelled Claude. "They's clear."

Kate went through the opening first and helped me out a moment later. Then, she took up the wet fullness of her skirts in both hands and we began running for our lives. I knew how good a tracker Claude was but we had a head start and they wouldn't be able to get to their horses right away. At least we now had a chance.

Twenty rods from the house, she pitched straight into a screen of tall rosebushes, coming out the other side with her beautiful green dress finally torn to pieces. She completed the job by removing her petticoats and ripping the hem of her dress off at the knees.

"Run, Jamie," she again commanded loudly. With that she was off across the terraced garden, hurtling over its low brick retaining walls like a fleeing deer.

The air temperature was far colder than the water we had come through, and looking back on it, I think the two of us soon might have frozen to death if we hadn't been running so hard.

We passed a gravel drive and then an open pasture before she led me into an old stand of piney woods. We could no longer move quickly but at the same time were completely masked from the wind along with anyone who was trying to pursue us. Kate never hesitated for a moment in the direction she followed and I never asked where we were going. Somehow, it was enough to be free and to know I now had an ally and friend to fight back at them.

There was no stopping to rest until Kate cleared the last of the piney branches and I found myself standing on bare ground again. By then we had covered a mile or more. Ahead of us were the shadowy walls of a whitewashed building.

Through the driving rain, I now saw it was another house, although by no means as grand as the Dandridge mansion.

More of a cottage, it was wood-framed and the walls were covered by vines of Virginia creeper. The yard was surrounded by a white picket fence.

"Our overseer lived here," said Kate, still out of breath. It came as a surprise for me to learn that as far as we had already come, we had not left the Dandridge holdings.

Inside, the air was musty and damp. The front room was low-ceilinged with long beams running the length of the house. It was filled with handmade country furniture. There must have been leaks upstairs because the walls were badly stained and in places the wallpaper had come loose and hung down toward the floor.

"It's been empty for more than two years," she said sadly, as if it were necessary to explain the damage. She found matches on a side table and carefully lit the wick of an oil lamp. It threw further light on the depressing scene.

"Come on. We need to find dry clothes," she said, heading up the stairs. In the first room we came to, she stripped the blankets off the bed, tossing one to me and wrapping herself in the other.

"If we hide here they will surely find us," I said, partly to keep my teeth from chattering. "The fat one is an old Indian tracker."

"We are not staying here," she replied calmly. "As soon as I'm ready, I'm going back."

The idea was so crazy I wasn't sure I had heard her correctly. Before I could speak, however, she was gone again. I followed her to another room that was apparently used for storage. A half-dozen turtle-backed trunks sat covered with dust on the floor.

"Those are my brothers' cases," she said, pointing to several against the far wall. I went to the first one and pried it open with my good hand. A whiff of camphor greeted my inspection along with layers of well-made boy's clothing. Although her brothers had long since outgrown these things, much of what was carefully packed away fit me perfectly, and with Kate's help I was soon buttoned into a warm collection of it.

Swiftly, she went through one of the other trunks, removed a selection of things, and disappeared down the hall. Five minutes later she was back, having changed into black corduroy riding britches, a heavy shirt, and light-colored calf-length boots. Her thick auburn hair was hidden under a wide-brimmed plantation hat.

"Damn these things," she said, while trying to adjust the tight-fitting woolen shirt.

Stuffing additional clothing into a canvas sack, she picked up the oil lamp and headed back downstairs.

"Let's have a look at your hand again," she said when we were in the kitchen.

The sock had truly begun to smell bad and I wasn't sure what we would find. I guess the fingers looked a lot worse than they felt but she never flinched when she saw them.

"Those bastards," was all she said. Using a sharp kitchen knife, she quickly trimmed away the last of the dead skin.

"Can you move them?" Kate asked, and I did.

"They're just very stiff."

"They will be that for as long as you live, I'm afraid," she said. After searching through the kitchen drawers, she came back with a jar labeled "Dr. Levin's All Purpose Youth Restorative and Cleansing Balm," and proceeded to coat my fingers with it. It felt like hot paste, and quickly set like hardened dough. Afterward, she wrapped the hand again with a piece of clean white cheesecloth and slid it into a large blue mitten she had brought from upstairs.

"I must go now, Jamie," she said, getting up and leaving the room.

In what must have been the overseer's office, she went straight to a large paneled cabinet that was built into the wall next to the fireplace. Sliding open the pocket door, she placed the lamp inside on a deep shelf.

"Go where?" I asked, although I already knew the answer.

"I'm going home," she replied fiercely. "I'm going to kill those men if I die trying."

I knew by then she meant every word. At the same time I tried to make her see reason.

"There are only two of us and five of them," I said.

She paused in her search and turned around, smiling.

"Thank you for including yourself, Jamie, but I must do this alone. Besides, one of them is sick and their leader is drunk," she said.

There was a fine breech-loading rifle in the recessed cabinet as well as a brace of pistols and shotguns.

"And I know exactly where to hide so I can shoot them when they go for their horses," Kate said with deadly calm as she brought the weapons out and laid them on the office desk.

"Why can't we go for help?" I said, but she just shook her head.

"Most of the places around here are deserted. Otherwise, we would find only women and children."

"We could go into Luray," I persisted.

"It would take hours on foot and by then they would have escaped. Don't think I'm not frightened, Jamie. I am. But I must make them pay for what they did to Franklin and my father. Can't you see I have to?"

I guess she was the most fearless girl who ever lived. Anyway, she wasn't about to listen to me. One way or another she was determined to avenge the murders.

"I'll go with you," I said and then began to shiver. I couldn't control it. She saw it all.

"I can't let you do that, Jamie. Besides, you're the only witness to what they did in case I—"

"You can't stop me from going with you," I said, "and I'm going."

She smiled at me again and took my good hand in hers. It was warm and soft.

"Have you ever fired a pistol, Jamie?" Kate asked me evenly.

"I have," I replied. "My grandfather taught me and I'm a good shot."

That was the truth although I didn't tell her we had to do it secretly. My father hated guns and refused to have one in the house until he joined the Confederate Army.

She removed a small six-shot revolver from its rack in the gun case, checked to see it was unloaded, and handed it to me. The top of the scrolled octagonal barrel was marked "Smith and Wesson, Springfield, Mass." Its grips were pure white ivory. The gun was light and easy to aim. I dry-fired it once to test the action.

"Could you handle something like this?" she asked. I nodded.

"Being able to aim and pull the trigger is quite different from killing a man," she went on. "Neither one of us has ever done murder before. Yesterday, I would have told you I never could."

The image of Corporal Blewitt's body being dragged through the snow behind Jupiter came into my mind and then fled again.

"I know what we have to do," I said, as she began to load the weapons.

We set out a little later, the wind lashing rain into our faces until we again entered the dense piney woods. Kate was weighted down with both the rifle and the double-barreled shotgun, which she carried inside a blanket roll on her back. I carried another shotgun along with the pistol and a sack of spare ammunition.

She may not have had Claude's tracking skills but she knew every inch of her father's vast estate. Another hour brought us to a point no more than thirty yards from the outbuilding where they had taken their horses, and around double that distance from the house.

Our hiding place was in the middle of a square of boxwoods that lined one side of the gravel drive. According to Kate it was a place she and her brothers had hollowed out as a secret lair when they were children. Not only was it a perfect ambush site, but we were almost completely protected from the wind and rain by the thick shrubbery above and around us.

Kate laid the loaded rifle and both shotguns in a row between the roots of the boxwoods that faced the outbuilding. It was around three in the morning by then and still too dark to see anything. No lights came from the house. For now at least, we were completely safe. She spread out the blanket roll and we lay down side by side.

"This may not be of comfort to you right now," she said softly, "but in any fight surprise is more than half the battle. At least that's what Jeb Stuart once told me."

I may not have looked persuaded because then she said, "You should also know I'm a crack marksman." In spite of the odds against us, I believed her.

Nevertheless, as it always did, my imagination began to run wild. In my mind's eye I saw Claude slithering around in that darkness with his Indian killer tricks. Even if he couldn't see us I was convinced he had yet the power to find us. I probably stunk bad enough for him to smell me by then.

Far more vivid images came to me of what Dex would do if he caught us again. I looked over at Kate who was lying close beside me. She was not suffering the same demons. Completely exhausted, she had fallen fast asleep, her sweet face calm in repose.

After all she had been through, I couldn't blame her. It was up to me to stand watch for the rest of that night and I did.

FOURTEEN

THE RAIN STOPPED sometime during the night, but it stayed frosty cold. When the first hint of dawn finally arrived, I happened to be staring at the house as it slowly came into view. A few minutes passed before I realized there was something wrong with what I was looking at. It took another five for me to figure out what it was.

There was no smoke coming from any of the chimneys.

I woke up Kate and told her.

"Why does that matter?" she asked groggily.

"You don't know those men. They're like spiders when it comes to the cold. If they were in there they would have a fire going."

"Where else could they be?"

To that question there was no immediate answer. We waited until it was completely light without seeing or hearing the slightest sign of their presence. Even more unusual, there were no sounds coming from the horses in the outbuilding where they had been liveried the previous afternoon.

Another thirty minutes went by before we agreed it was time to act. Kate crawled on her belly to a point under the boxwoods where she was completely screened from the house. Slipping from her hiding place, she crept to the nearest window while I covered her with one of the shotguns. She stood up to glance inside for a moment and then dropped back down. Returning to the cover of the boxwoods, she crawled back to me.

"The horses are gone," she whispered breathlessly.

Together, we left our hiding place and cautiously went to the window of the shed. Raising it open, we stepped inside to find that, sure enough, it was empty. Not only were the horses gone but all the rest of the men's gear as well.

We talked over what to do next. There was no alternative but to explore the house, but we could not approach it without being seen. If it was a trap and one of them had remained behind, we would be perfect targets.

With each step toward the mansion house, I expected to hear the crack of gunfire, but we reached the glass-paneled doors at the end of the garden without misadventure, and found them unlocked. An arched corridor ran the length of that wing of the house, and we slowly went along it, looking in each room as we came. Most of them were shuttered, as silent and dark as tombs.

In the library, the massive Christmas tree was now tipped over on its side, most of its handmade ceramic and glass decorations smashed underfoot. Kate stood rigid with anger, gazing down at the shattered family treasures. My own eyes were drawn to the small river of blood that had poured out of her family's servant and was now drying to a rusty brown on the wide-planked floor. I could smell its corrupt sweetness over the clean scent of the fresh-cut spruce tree.

Our private thoughts were broken up by a low moaning noise that came from somewhere above us. At first I thought it might be just a sigh of wind in the chimney, but when it was repeated I recognized the sound for a human cry. Kate and I walked upstairs, pistols at the ready.

We found Royal Bevinger lying on a huge four-poster bed in one of the bedrooms, and a gruesome sight it was. The canopy of the bed was lined with embroidered lace and the room was painted in tones of peach and lime. It contrasted wildly with the red-soaked bedclothes under which his body was lying.

He was turned away from us, still oblivious to our presence. When we came around the other side of the bed to face him, he looked up at us with burning feverish eyes and tried vainly to smile.

"They cleared out an hour after you escaped," he said through clenched teeth. "Thought you would raise half the countryside before you came back."

"Where have they gone?" Kate demanded.

"Sudley Springs," he said, focusing on me. "They figure you're headed there too, Jamie."

A spasm of pain shook his spare body under the bloody spread. "Captain McQuade knows within a quarter mile where the gold is buried," he continued. "They'll be waiting for you."

"If that is where they are going, then that is where I am going," said Kate.

"Cole tried to protect me from them," he went on. "Dex wanted to kill me outright after you escaped, but Claude said I was dying anyway, which was the truth. Been coughing up blood for weeks . . . But Dex came back just before they left to finish the job with his knife . . . too weak to stop him."

"Now there are only four," said Kate without a hint of pity in her voice.

"All for the best," said Royal Bevinger. "Never should have gone with them."

"Why did you?" I asked.

"Wanted to rebuild our farm after Hunter's men burned it out last summer. Mary had no place to go after that. Don't know where she is—"

Another spasm took him and he cried out in agony. When he spoke again, the words came much faster, as if he knew the end was coming.

"I'm sorry, Jamie. Tell your father that at the end I tried to do right by you."

Kate continued to stare at him as if he were a feral dog.

"Captain McQuade is a good man, Jamie," he said then.

"I will see him dead," came back Kate, as she turned and stalked out of the room. Royal Bevinger seemed to take no notice.

"He never had any intention of going back for that gold until after the letter came," he said, coughing hard enough to shake apart. Another gout of blood poured out of his mouth and he finally lay back, exhausted.

"The letter?" I said. It was necessary to repeat the words again before he was able to continue.

"His wife and both daughters," he said. "All dead within a day of each other from scarlet fever . . . After that nothing mattered . . . Then this winter he said he had a use for the gold."

"What use?" I blurted out, but as I did, his body uncoiled and his clenched hands slid away from his belly. Once more, he struggled to raise his head from the pillow, as if he still had something important to say. Then, the death agony left his face and his body relaxed. I again saw the kind, pleasant features of the man I had met so often before the war. Still standing beside the bed, I silently offered him my gratitude for saving us from the others.

Kate was no longer in the house when I went to look for her. I found her in the carriage shed, kneeling in the dirt beside the corpse of her father, her hands clasped together in prayer. She had covered both his body and that of their Negro servant with white muslin sheets. Laddy was lying all by himself near the hitching post. He was facing toward me, with the same child-like, bewildered smile frozen on his mouth.

Kate stood up and turned to me, saying, "It's time to go, Jamie."

"To Sudley Springs?" I asked, and she nodded.

"First, we'll need horses," she said. "Follow me."

She headed straight toward the boxwoods to retrieve the rest of the guns. We then repacked the clothes and firearms we had brought from the overseer's cottage in our bedrolls. She took nothing from the mansion house that had been home all her life.

I guess I would have followed her anywhere by then. Already, I felt there was a true bond between us. It was more than a friendship. Although I had only known her a short time, I knew I could trust her with my life, just as I was ready to give up my own for hers if it came to that.

Just the fact of walking beside her put resolution in my heart and strength in my legs. Right then her large green eyes were full of sorrow and I knew she was remembering her life that once was, and which was now gone forever.

But Kate's spirit seemed to find release as she walked, as if being in the open air freed her from the prison of her tragic memories. Her energy seemed boundless, and aside from the red glow that suffused the alabaster skin of her cheeks, she showed no sign of the hard exertion required to cross those steep foothills and rocky fields.

At that time I was already beginning to feel poorly. Not only had I been up all the previous night, but there were the many days and nights exposed to the raw elements. I would have been left far behind had she not slowed her light-footed pace to accommodate me. Whenever we came to a difficult passage, she took my hand in hers, and the strength that I felt flowing inside her gave me the energy to go on.

As we walked, I told Kate everything that had happened to me, starting with the night Corporal Blewitt came to Port Republic, and how I had followed him to the graveyard. When I reached the part of telling her how I had killed him, she actually stopped in her tracks and turned to me wide-eyed, as if not sure whether I could be telling the truth. After looking into my eyes for a long moment, she nodded once and I knew she believed me.

I then spoke about Major de Monfort and how he had saved me, first at Trumbo's and later on at New Market. Finally, I related what took place after I was caught by the gang. The last thing I told her about was the map and my genuine belief that I knew where to find the gold. To this news she exhibited not the slightest interest. It was plain her only goal was to catch up to the men who had killed her father.

A little more than two hours of fast walking brought us to a steep hill, at the bottom of which was a quaint old village. According to Kate, it had once been the busy intersection of two stagecoach lines that no longer existed. Below us I could now see a cluster of cabins, stores, and cottages filling the space on both sides of the road. We had to cross a rickety plank bridge to get there, and as we passed over it, I saw that the stream beneath us was raging far and wide over its banks.

"I've never seen it like this, even in early spring," I said as we passed over the crossing.

"It's all the snow and rain we've had," she replied. "The ground cannot absorb any more water."

As we approached the center of the settlement, I could see an open square dotted with ancient trees. Many of the buildings in the village faced onto it. Kate began to walk faster.

"Helen Kerfoot lives here," she said, as if that should mean something to me.

After crossing the park, she headed straight for a large white clapboard house that dominated the buildings on the other side of the square. She mounted the stairs of the front porch two at a time, and without bothering to knock, opened the unlocked door and called out, "Helen!"

Thirty seconds later, the hall was filled with a small army of women and children, all talking at once. They came from every direction and engulfed us.

"Who are you?" demanded one.

"Is that you, Katharine?" asked another.

"Where have you come from?" said a third.

When Kate removed the planter's hat, her thick chestnut mane spilled down around her shoulders.

"Why, it *is* Katharine," said the second woman.

"Helen!" Kate called out again over the tumult.

A massive figure suddenly appeared at the head of the stairs. Her long curly hair was pure silver and she had a face like George Washington.

"Katharine Dandridge," she called out in a booming voice, "you look as if you've come straight from the trenches at Richmond."

I saw her eyes swing over to me. With a mocking tone to her voice, she added, "And who is this ragamuffin you've dragged in with you?" Then, she saw the look of distress on Kate's face and right away her manner changed.

"Why, child, what is the matter?" she cried, almost charging down the stairs toward us. For all her size, she moved very nimbly.

"I need to talk to you alone, Helen," said Kate.

"Make room, make room," boomed Mrs. Kerfoot as she led us through the crush in the corridor. "If you're going to have the vapors, Addie, don't do it here," she barked at a thin woman who was holding a lace-trimmed handkerchief to her nose.

We moved along in the wake of the big woman. Each room we passed appeared to have been converted for sleeping. Straw-filled mattresses lay everywhere on the floor. When we reached the winter kitchen at the back of the house, Mrs. Kerfoot closed the door behind her.

A gigantic orange cat lay curled up on the wood box near the stove. The big, warm room was empty of people just then, but filled with the savory aroma of their Christmas baking.

"Helen, this is my friend Jamie Lockhart," said Kate. "He needs something to eat." Mrs. Kerfoot shifted her worried glance to me for a moment and then back to Kate.

"We can fill that cavity," she said with a terse smile. Four crusty fruit pies were cooling on a pine harvest table near the stove. As she picked up a bread knife and began to cut me a piece, she said, "Now, tell me what has happened, Katharine."

"Father and Franklin have both been murdered," she said, simply. The big woman's head jerked back as if she had been slapped, and the knife fell right out of her hand.

"Oh, Sweet Jesus," said Helen Kerfoot, her deep voice turning into a low-pitched groan.

"Do you still have those horses hidden at Peak's?" Kate asked then.

"Yes. They are still there," Mrs. Kerfoot replied.

"Could I have the loan of two of them?"

"Of course, Katharine, but surely that can wait until the arrangements—"

"I need them right now, Helen," replied Kate. "As for the burial arrangements, I would ask you to see to them. Father and Franklin are both lying in the carriage shed."

"If you haven't already notified the authorities," said Mrs. Kerfoot, "there is a Yankee provost in Luray I have dealt with who is not a complete savage."

"Do as you see fit, Helen."

"Where are you going?"

"After the murderer," said Kate.

I expected Mrs. Kerfoot to have a fit about the idea, but it didn't seem to come as a surprise. I gathered she had some past experience in dealing with Kate. The next words bore that out.

"I know how willful and headstrong you can be when you set your mind on something, Katharine, but for God's sake, please listen to reason. Leave the apprehension of this brigand to people who—"

"I will not take unnecessary risks, Helen," she said.

I did not point out the fact that there were four of them, not one. At that moment, the far door of the kitchen burst open and I was surrounded again in bedlam.

They were army wives, most of them, and all invited by Mrs. Kerfoot, to stay with her for the duration. They came from as far as Martinsburg, and were desperately anxious to know what was happening at the front.

"What news have you?" shouted the woman who was now standing right over me.

"Have you come from Richmond?" demanded a second. Before I could answer, a lady who was about to give child said, "Are they still holding?"

"Let him alone. He looks like he's starving," said another, finally cutting me a wedge of warm apple pie. It was fresh from the oven and as good as anything I've ever tasted. While devouring it, I tried to listen to Kate's conversation with Mrs. Kerfoot.

Over the din around me, the only words I heard were from Mrs. Kerfoot. That was because she raised her voice to say, "Place your faith in a just God, my child." A little later, I heard her declare, "This isn't about choosing a beau, Katharine. This is pure madness."

A little boy joined me at the table. He couldn't have been more than five years old but his eyes were as grave as a new widow.

"You been to the war?"

"Part of it," I said, truthfully.

"Will it end soon?"

"Soon enough," I said.

"My pa went to win the war," he said. "You think he'll be back soon?"

"I'm sure he will," I said, and hoped I was right.

The conversation between Kate and Mrs. Kerfoot ended. Kate came over to me then and whispered, "She is sending her hired man for the horses. He should be back here in an hour and we'll leave right away. In the meantime, finish eating. I'm going to have a bath and then put together what we need to take."

"Who is Mrs. Kerfoot?" I asked.

"She is my great-aunt and was my mother's best friend. Helen has outlasted three husbands and raised nine children. Since the war began, she has taken in half the destitute army wives in the valley."

After I finished eating, one of the women took me to a room where someone had brought a pitcher of hot water and a precious bar of soap. She poured the water into a basin for me and then left the room. I stripped off my clothes and, using my good hand, tried my best to wash myself. After putting on clean socks and underclothes, I felt much better.

Kate was in earnest conversation with Mrs. Kerfoot again in the front parlor when I came downstairs. The rest of the women were gathered like pecking hens in the hallway, watching and waiting.

As I entered the room, Kate was saying, "Someone needs to get word to his mother that he is all right."

"I will take care of it," said Helen Kerfoot. "The telegraph wires have been down for weeks, which is why they are so nervous. If necessary I will send Jonah to Port Republic to deliver the message himself. She must be out of her mind with worry."

Kate asked me to compose a short letter and I sat down at a table in front of the window with pen and ink. It struck me that telling her any of the story at that point would only increase her anxiety. Instead, this is what I wrote:

Dear Mother,
    Please do not worry about me. I am fine and have made

a very good friend. I hope you are all right and that you have heard from Father by now. I will be home soon. Love, Jamie.

As I finished writing, the clatter of horses' hooves could be heard on the road outside. Mrs. Kerfoot took the note and sealed it in an embossed cream-colored envelope. Kate was already in her coat and heading toward the backyard of the house. When I got outside, there were two horses tethered to the large iron ring on the stone hitching post.

"They're the best two I have left," said Mrs. Kerfoot. "The gray is Arabian and the roan is out of Moon Dancer. They will take you a long way."

"Thank you, Helen," said Kate as she carefully examined their legs and feet.

"Promise me, child, you will come back to us. Don't take foolish chances."

"I promise," she said with such a confident smile that Mrs. Kerfoot might have even believed it was true. At least until we were gone.

The hired man finished strapping our bedrolls and two bulging food sacks onto the saddles. Then, Kate was up on the gray. I mounted the roan. He felt young and powerful and ready to run.

With a smooth, practiced tug on the reins, Kate backed her horse from the hitching post and turned him around.

"God bless you, Katharine," said Helen Kerfoot, her booming voice reduced to little more than a croak.

"Goodbye, Helen," said Kate, spurring the stallion forward out of the yard. I followed behind her, looking back just once as we turned onto the village square.

Mrs. Kerfoot was holding one hand to her face. The other was clutching the hitching post. The hired man was running toward her as if he thought she was about to fall down.

A FLOCK OF CROWS called out to us from the tops of the spare, leafless trees. Not far above them, low dark clouds threatened snow again, although so far it was holding off. The country was as lonely as any I had gone through since leaving home, and most of the small dwellings we saw along the way appeared abandoned.

For the first part of the journey we didn't see another human being. Kate had decided to avoid the well-traveled trunk road that led up to Thornton Gap in the Blue Ridge Mountains. It was the principal connection point between the Luray Valley and the rest of Virginia to the east. She thought McQuade and his band might be lying in wait for us along that route.

Instead Kate was aiming to cross the mountains at a place called the Pinnacle, which was a four-thousand-foot promontory to the south of Thornton Gap. She had once explored it with her brothers on a camping trip before the war. Beyond that peak, Kate said there was a narrow trail we could traverse down to the Virginia plain, where the road through Sperryville would eventually take us to Sudley Springs.

To get there, we followed a succession of cramped country lanes that finally brought us to the first sharp incline of a forest path that led up toward the windswept, blue-black mountain.

From out of the gloom ahead of us a thin, quavering voice cried out, "Halt and be recognized."

We reined up and waited to see who was there. Slowly, three riders emerged from the dark of the forest that hemmed in both sides of the road. The one in front was an old man wearing a tri-cornered hat and an antiquated blue military coat with great gold epaulets on each shoulder. The second man was even more wizened than the first, while the last was a lumpy-faced boy of twelve or thirteen.

The second man's head was covered by a piece of green tent material, around two feet square, which was tied by a length of rope beneath his chin. He and the boy both had yellow strips of cloth fastened around their right arms. All three of them were carrying smoothbore muskets.

"I am Colonel Leonidas Chew," said the one in the uniform. "What is your business here?"

I now saw he was walleyed and wasn't sure which one of us he was talking to.

"My name is Katharine Dandridge."

"One of Judge Dandridge's brood?"

"He is my father," said Kate, raising her head proudly.

"You've got his high-and-mighty ways, I see. All right, men," he ordered. "Lower your arms."

"Why are you guarding this road?" she asked.

"I have the honor to command the only Confederate military forces between here and Sperryville," he declared solemnly.

"Hawshit," snorted the other old man, who was riding a swaybacked mule.

Ignoring his subordinate, Colonel Chew said, "We're holding this part of the valley until President Davis sees fit to send back the Army of the Shenandoah. In the meantime we're on the lookout for the Yankee trash that stole my last three hogs."

"Is the pass clear beyond the pinnacle?"

"Far as I know," he said. "Where are you headed?"

"Richmond," she lied.

"Then you should be gratified to learn I have recently received word that General Hardee is bringing his army north to join forces with General Lee. Together they will give Grant the licking he deserves and drive him north out of Virginia."

"Hawshit," repeated the other man, while spewing out a mouthful of tobacco juice.

"Careful, Private Horner, or I'll have you bucked for disobedience."

"You and who else?" said the other, completely unrepentant.

When we left them on the road, they were still arguing, although the boy had already gone, having announced that his mother would whale him good and proper if he didn't get right home to finish his chores. They were the last people we saw that day.

Toward dusk we finally reached the Pinnacle. Kate led me straight to the place where she and her brothers had camped before the war. It was sheltered from the wind by massive boulders on both sides and there was a declivity in the rocks where we could lay out our sleeping blankets in full protection from the elements, while still enjoying a view of the countryside below.

As darkness settled over the plain to the east, I could see the twinkling lights of a small settlement that Kate told me was Sperryville. One mile beyond it was a cluster of bivouac fires which revealed the presence of a large military force. Based on the number of points of fire, I could estimate that more than a thousand soldiers were encamped there. In a small way it reminded me of the night before the Battle of Port Republic when there were so many campfires in the fields around Lynwood it was almost like daylight.

Then, I wondered how many of those men in Jackson's old army were still alive after all the bloody battles that had been fought in the years since. Not many, I guessed. For the thousandth time I prayed that my father would be one of the lucky ones to be spared.

With my bad hand, I wasn't much good for any real work, but I did find a large pocket of dead leaves where the wind had blown them into a cleft in the rocks and spread them out under our blankets. I also gathered enough dead wood to keep up a good blaze through the long bitter night to come.

For supper, we ate the roasted ham on thick slices of baked bread that had been packed for us by the women before we left. Later, the wind came up, spraying the sparks from our fire wildly into the air. That was when I asked Kate why Helen Kerfoot had called her willful and headstrong. In consequence, she stared long and hard into the flames.

"I was a great disappointment to my mother," she said finally. "When I was growing up, she always wanted me to be a proper young lady. All I ever wanted was to be like my brothers. Running free. Riding off to places like this."

"A tomboy?" I said.

"Yes. A tomboy."

I got up and added several large branches to the fire. Kate remained motionless.

"And then when I did realize I enjoyed female things," she went on, "I truly disappointed her by falling in love with a boy who wasn't suitable. It was right after the start of the war. He didn't believe in the cause. I almost ran off with him anyway."

I was afraid to change her mood by asking another question, and just waited for her to continue.

"He was the first boy who had the courage to ask me to dance," she said, laughing out loud. "It may have been the first night I ever wore a gown to a party."

The carefree smile on her face slowly disappeared as if some less hospitable ghost had invaded her memory.

"It was his unfortunate destiny to believe heart and soul in the preservation of the Union," she said.

I wondered who he was and what he was like. I wondered what it was about him that had made her fall in love with him.

Then she laughed again.

"What?" I demanded.

"He called me his beautiful Rebel."

"You loved a Yankee?" I said, shocked.

"No, he was a Virginian," she said.

"Where is he now?"

"He was killed in the second year of the war."

"Oh," I said. "Well, at least your mother must have been sorry for having doubted him."

"No, Jamie. You see, he was a captain in the Union Army when he died at Seven Pines."

That ended our conversation for a while. When I looked up from the fire again I saw she was crying.

"It's no good," she said finally, her voice trailing off.

"What?" I asked.

"As terrible as war is, I never imagined it would be like this."

I wanted so much to comfort her then but was numbed at the enormity of everything she had lost.

"Please talk," she said.

"About what?"

"Anything. Just talk."

There was nothing I could think of to say that didn't sound stupid.

"What about you, Jamie? Have you ever fallen in love?"

I felt the blood rushing into my face and turned away.

"A man of secrets, I see," she said with a gentle smile. And then, "You've had to grow up very fast, haven't you?"

"No more than anyone else," I said.

We both stared into the fire again.

"Well, let's turn in before I start pouring out the rest of my family scandals," she said.

That night alone with Kate at the Pinnacle was the soundest sleep I have enjoyed from the time Corporal Blewitt came to this very day. Maybe I should put rocks in my bed from now on.

SIXTEEN

I AWOKE SHORTLY before dawn, hoping above all it would be a day without snow or rain. Miraculously, the sky to the east was clear that morning, although when I looked to the north, I could see another mass of low dark clouds surging toward us to blot out the heavens.

Nevertheless, in those few minutes I found pleasure in feeling the fragile rays of the winter sun on my face as I gazed out for miles from the summit of the Blue Ridge across the vast Virginia plain. There was no way to see that far, but I looked to the southeast and imagined my father at that very moment enjoying the warmth of the same sun from wherever he lay in the trenches around Richmond.

Before breaking camp, Kate and I enjoyed a breakfast of tea and fire-toasted corn bread. Then, she saddled the horses and we were off again.

The trip down the mountain was uneventful, although every creek and stream we crossed seemed to have overflowed its banks in its boiling flight to the plain below. I was saddened at the knowledge it would cause flooding for the people who lived in the bottomlands and add to their trials in this last bitter season of the war.

It was near midday when we reached the foothills of the Blue Ridge. There, the mountain trail merged into a forest road that ran in the easterly direction we needed to follow. By then, the sky had gotten very dark again.

"We should be in Sperryville in another twenty minutes," said Kate, shivering in the harsh wind that presaged more rain or snow.

We were still in dense forest when off in the distance I saw a white church spire rising above the tops of the trees. As we rode closer, the squared-off steeple below it came into view, and then the little wood-frame church itself. It stood all alone in a glade that had recently been hacked out of the forest. Raw tree stumps still covered most of the cleared land that separated it from the surrounding woods. It must have had a small congregation, because the building looked barely large enough to hold the choir of our Methodist church in Port Republic.

I remember wondering if it was Sunday because a group of maybe fifteen horsemen were sitting their mounts in a rough circle around the two oak trees that marked the entrance to the churchyard.

Then to my horror I realized what was happening. They were all watching a man who was hanging by the neck from one of the trees. It must have just occurred because as we drew nearer I saw that the hanged man was not yet dead. Even though his hands were tied behind his back, his legs had been left free and he was now kicking out wildly as if still convinced there was a chance to run away from the rope.

By the time we came abreast of the group, he had finally finished his grotesque dance and now hung limp. There was a feed sack over his head but it didn't hide the bright blue uniform of a Federal soldier.

The horsemen surrounding him all appeared to be dressed

in raggedy combinations of castoff clothing, although I could now see there was yet another soldier in blue as well. He sat on his horse between two men in butternut-gray. Like the other one, his hands were bound behind his back. He had on a wide-brimmed black hat that was rakishly tilted to one side. At his neck he wore a red silk bandanna.

I guess he was around twenty years old and the type people call a lady's man. His gold-trimmed cavalry uniform looked custom-fitted and it clung tightly to his slim handsome figure. His eyes were a striking blue.

Knowing what was about to happen to him, he just stared hollowly out of the dark, clean-shaved face. At the same time he betrayed no fear. He sat his horse calmly, as if resigned to accept whatever fate had in store for him.

The leader of the Confederates was younger than the Yankee. He was bareheaded with long corn-colored hair and a freckled boyish face. The only thing old about him were his eyes. They were stone-cold gray and there were wrinkly pouches under them like he hadn't slept in a while.

Nevertheless, he seemed completely at ease, puffing on a hand-rolled cigarette and sitting his fine palomino with one leg casually extended across the horse's neck. Two deerskin holsters hung from his saddle horn, each one containing a big bone-handled pistol.

"What did these men do?" asked Kate.

"I suggest you leave that be and ride along, ma'am," said the leader politely. He had sergeant's stripes sewed on the sleeves of his patched brown tunic.

"But these men are your prisoners," she came back. "This one's just a boy."

"He's old enough to be wearin' that pretty uniform," said the sergeant with an easy smile.

"Whom do I have the privilege of addressing?" said Kate in her courtliest manner.

"Sergeant Downy, ma'am . . . Mosby's Partisan Rangers."

"I happen to know your commander, Sergeant. Colonel Mosby is a fine soldier."

"Yes, ma'am."

"I cannot believe he would sanction what you are doing here."

"Well, you could take that up with him," said the sergeant. "But he ain't here right now."

One of his men snickered at that.

"I think you should treat this man as the obvious prisoner of war he is," persisted Kate, who was used to getting her own way.

"I'm sorry, Miss . . ."

"Dandridge. Katharine Dandridge."

"I'm sorry, Miss Dandridge, but I don't care a bucket of warm spit about what you think, beggin' your pardon, ma'am," he said.

Then one of the others said, "Don't you waste no tears on the likes of him. His people murdered three of our men in Front Royal this week past. No trial. Just strung them up like sides of beef in the town square and left 'em hanging there with sign boards on their chest. We're just payin' back in kind."

"An eye for'n eye," said another.

"I don't know anything about any murderers," declared the young Yankee. "I've just come from Winchester."

"See what he told ya?" yelled someone. "One of Sheridan's scum."

"Who are you?" Kate asked the Federal directly.

"I'm Private Johnny Bellayne, ma'am. Fourth Pennsylvania Cavalry, currently attached to the staff of General Gouverneur Warren. I'm carrying dispatches to the general at Fifth Corps headquarters in Petersburg."

"You *was* carrying dispatches," corrected the hard-faced boy on the horse next to him.

"Come on, Jeff, let's git it over with," demanded another. "Could be a Yank patrol through here anytime."

The Federal spoke up again. "They're bound to do it, ma'am, now that they've done for my friend. Thank you for trying, but will you do one thing for me? Could you take a note to my mother?"

"If Sergeant Downy allows me," she said, looking straight at him with eyes of contempt.

"Go rat ahead," he said with another smile.

"There's a pencil and paper in my pocket," said the Federal.

The boy on the horse next to him removed a small bound diary from his shirt and tossed it to Kate. Johnny Bellayne then told her the name and address of his mother in Lancaster, Pennsylvania, and she wrote it down.

The next thing he said was, "Please don't tell her how I died here . . . Just say . . . just say it was in a good cause."

"What cause?" someone muttered. "Wagin' war on women and children?"

"Shut up, Darce," said Sergeant Downy.

"Tell her I know I will see her and Pa in heaven," Johnny Bellayne went on.

The crazy thing about it all was he seemed as calm right then as if he were just planning to take a trip to a distant land instead of facing a horrible death.

When he was finished, he said, "Thank you, Miss Dandridge. I'm at peace now." Then he fell silent.

Kate's eyes were like green fire again.

"You've got your letter, lady," said the sergeant. "Now ride along."

"No I won't," she said with passion. "If you're so proud of what you are doing then you should have no concern if I watch . . . Or is it that you would rather have no witnesses?"

"Hangin' ain't no fit sight for a woman," said one of the others.

"Suit yourself, Miss Dandridge," said Sergeant Downy. "Get him ready, Lon."

The Confederate led Johnny Bellayne's horse up until it was directly under the second oak tree. A length of stout rope was already hanging from one of the limbs. It ended in an open noose. The other end was tied around the trunk of the tree.

When one of them tried to drape a feed sack over the Yankee's head, he balked and tried to weave away.

"Don't," he said, for the first time defiant.

Sergeant Downy nodded once and the man dropped the bag to the ground. Then, he plucked off Johnny Bellayne's wide-brimmed hat and threw it to one of the others, who promptly tried it on and pronounced it a good fit. By then, the noose was around the Yankee's neck and drawn tight.

Until that moment I couldn't believe it would really happen. Then, one of them grabbed the reins of his horse while the others backed their own mounts away.

That's when Kate cried out, "What is wrong with you men? What has happened to you? Has the Confederate army lost all sense of humanity?"

None of them but Sergeant Downy would look her in the eye. One after another the others all stared down at the ground.

"Where is your honor?" she called out. "Let this poor boy go!"

"Don't preachify to us about honor," snarled Sergeant Downy. "Talk to your Yankee friends about that. They started this kind of war."

"That makes you no better than them," she shouted back.

"So be it," he said, coaxing his horse toward the Yankee.

"I will personally report what you're about to do here to Congressman Boteler," Kate shouted.

"When you see the congressman tell him we have things under control in this part of Virginia," said the sergeant as he reached the Federal's side.

I took one last look at Johnny Bellayne. Even though he

was trying not to show it, I knew he was scared because he had bitten down hard enough on his lower lip so that blood was running out through his teeth.

Now, Sergeant Downy was leaning way out of the saddle. Raising his reins over his head, he whipped the hindquarters of the Federal's horse and it bolted forward. I think the Yankee's neck must have snapped right away because, unlike his friend, he never struggled at all as he entered the life eternal.

For at least a minute, Kate didn't take her eyes off his face. Tears welled up in her eyes and began to run slowly down her cheeks. Still, she didn't look away, even when one of the Confederates began trying to drag off the Yankee's boots.

"That'll do," Sergeant Downy said harshly.

"But they's brand-new," complained the man, who was barefoot on the icy ground. In spite of his plea, the boots stayed on the corpse.

The horsemen quickly formed up to move out. Two of the Confederates had already claimed the sleek Yankee mounts as prizes of war. They took their own sorry animals in tow as the rest of the men began to clatter away down the road. At that moment, Kate called out after them, "I'll see you in Hell, Sergeant."

He stopped his horse for a moment and looked back at her.

"I truly hope that ain't your destination, Miss Dandridge," he said with a final boyish grin. Making an elegant bow from the saddle, Sergeant Downy turned the big palomino around and rode away.

SEVENTEEN

BEFORE RIDING ON, we cut the dead Yankees down and hastily tried to arrange their bodies in a dignified way. Of course, there was nothing dignified about the way they had died, or about what the Yankees would do next after they found them lying by the road in front of the church.

It would mean even harsher retaliation against our people. Then the new Yankee reprisals would almost certainly lead to more violent episodes of hatred and murder. Where would it all end? I wondered.

As we rode into the outskirts of Sperryville, the gale that had threatened all day finally unleashed its fury upon us. Driven by the north wind, the rain pelted our faces and slowed the horses to a walk.

Much of the town lay in ruins. It had been the site of many skirmishes and repeated occupations by one side or the other since the start of the war, because it lay right at the entrance to the Blue Ridge in that part of Virginia. Most of the shops were boarded up, probably because no one had any goods left to sell. We continued through the town until finally I saw a glimmer of lights coming from a building set back on high ground about fifty feet from the road.

It appeared to be a barn that had been converted into an eating and drinking establishment. Seeing all the horses with U.S. Army saddles tied to the hitching rails out front, I concluded it had been set up to accommodate Yankee soldiers. We decided to stop there until the rain abated.

There was a small shed in the rear and we left the horses there, loosening the girths of their saddles, and letting them share a half bale of hay that Kate purchased from the slack-jawed stableboy for fifty dollars Confederate. As we were leaving the shed, I noticed it seemed to be overrun with cats. They were everywhere, lolling in each nook and cranny. I had never seen so many in one place before and wondered who the Good Samaritan might be who could afford to keep them so fat and contented at that point in the war.

The inn was made up of just one huge room with a packed earthen floor. A third of it was topped with what had once been the hayloft. The whole place was now filled with hand-hewn log tables and benches. About thirty Yankee soldiers were scattered around the room, most of them drinking whiskey. The air was hazy with tobacco smoke.

Seeing Kate at the door, the jowly innkeeper waddled over and escorted us to a table off to one side. With an air of apology, he quietly informed us the soldiers were all part of a cavalry regiment billeted at the fortified encampment nearby. It was then I remembered seeing their fires from our campsite on the Pinnacle the night before.

Although none of the soldiers attempted to talk to us after we sat down, several of them cast admiring glances at Kate, which she completely ignored. They were in a noisy and excited mood. Part of it obviously stemmed from what they were drinking in such large quantities. But that wasn't all of it. They were just plain happy. The men sitting near our table were trying to make wagers that the war would be over in a month. They couldn't find anyone to take the bet. I knew their spirits would not have been so gay if they could have seen Johnny Bellayne at that moment, lying in the mud a few miles to the west of us.

The smell of frying meat from the kitchen was making my mouth water and I asked Kate if I could order an early supper while we were waiting. She right away agreed, and ten minutes later a slovenly girl in a greasy apron brought me out a tin plate heaped with stewed turnips and some chunks of gray, gristly meat. As hungry as I was, I turned to it with greedy relish.

"From what I hear," shouted one of the soldiers across the room, "if they dig them trenches any deeper around Richmond, the whole city is going to disappear down a giant sinkhole."

His comment was met with boisterous laughter.

"I betcha a sawbuck we'll be mustered out in two months," called out another. Again, there were no takers.

"What is this here meat?" demanded one of the soldiers who had just been served at another table.

"Venison," said the innkeeper. "Fresh kill."

"Mighty tough chewin'," said the soldier.

"You should count your blessings," said one of his mates. "They say the Reb army is eating cats and dogs." With that the whole place erupted again in laughter.

The innkeeper was laughing right along with the soldiers, but as he turned away from them, his eyes happened to lock onto mine. Unseen by the Yankees, he arched his eyebrows at me as if we were sharing a private joke at their expense.

I made the mistake then of looking down at the gray chunks of meat left on my own plate. An instant later my stomach began to heave as I remembered all the cats in the shed.

"Why don't you finish your supper?" asked Kate. "You looked as famished as a wolf a few minutes ago."

"I guess I lost my appetite."

"Do you want me to wrap it for you?" she asked, and I just shook my head.

The rain showed no sign of slackening, but as time passed, Kate began to worry about what would happen if Johnny Bellayne's body was discovered while we were still in Sperryville. There would have been a lot of questions for strangers like us.

Then, I reminded her of the man that Major de Monfort had told me about beyond Massies Glen. From where we were at that point, his house was no more than five or six miles to the east. She agreed it made sense for us to head there right away, even if only for the duration of the storm.

A little more than an hour later, we passed through Massies Glen. Unlike Sperryville, it appeared to be untouched by the fighting. Somehow, the war had left its brightly painted cottages and houses in peace. Each building along the main street had its own fenced-in lawn and garden, and most of them were gaily lit for the Christmas holiday. It was like a stab to my heart as I thought of my mother alone at home, not knowing where either my father or I was this night.

One of the houses sat right at the edge of the street. Through the windows I could see a family decorating their Christmas tree in the front parlor. It seemed so warm and inviting. A man my father's age was attaching sprigs of holly to the mantelpiece. I wondered what they were having for dinner and saw in my mind a great roast goose and a huge bowl of mashed potatoes swimming in giblet gravy.

Then I looked over at Kate, who was gazing in the same window with desolate eyes. Seeing me, she immediately turned away. We silently rode on through the pitiless rain.

A mile past Massies Glen, I began to look ahead for signs of the settlement named Calvary. After we went on for another fifteen minutes without seeing any sign of habitation, I began to question whether Major de Monfort might have given me wrong information in the confusion of our parting.

Kate was the first one to see light in the distance. At first, it appeared to be moving back and forth in a horizontal line. As we came closer I realized it was a man standing in the middle of the road waving a railroad lantern.

"Bridge is gone," he shouted over the shrieking wind. "You have to go back."

"We need to get to Calvary," I shouted to him.

"Only way to get there now is to cross the stream about a hundred yards up that way," he said, pointing to a track that headed north. "You'll see where the bank's worn down at the ford, but it's more'n likely too deep to cross."

We thanked him and began to turn our horses north.

"Who you got to see?" he called out.

"Man named Gamage," I yelled back.

"Gamage, you say?"

"That's right."

"You family of his?"

"No," I shouted.

"I don't mean to tell you nothin'," he shouted back, obviously wanting to tell us something.

"Yes?" said Kate.

"Man's crazy as a coot."

The words gave us pause.

"Do you know where he lives?" I finally asked.

"Highland Manor. Yankees burned most of it in sixty-three. Now it's falling down around him . . . You can't see it from the pike. Only way you'll know you're there is when you're nigh on thirty rods past the bridge . . . look for the break in the trees on your right."

"Thank you," called out Kate as she nudged the Arabian forward.

"You jes remember what I told you, lady."

"Thank you," she repeated.

"Don't mean to tell you nothin'," he shouted again as we rode off.

We followed the track to the ford he had described and

stopped our horses to survey the crossing. Even though we couldn't see it, I could tell that the stream was no longer a stream. It was rumbling wildly past in a great crescendo of noise. In the darkness there was no way to tell just how wide the fording place had become, but compared to the cataract I had ridden through above New Market Gap, it didn't look all that difficult to cross.

We had no choice but to go forward. By now, the Yankees were sure to have found the bodies of Johnny Bellayne and his friend, and were probably sending patrols in every direction to arrest anyone who might have information about the murders. If we headed back toward Sperryville we were bound to be taken.

I found Kate's warm hand clasping my own. A moment later, we spurred our horses and headed into the maelstrom. At first, the streambed stayed shallow and I thought we would make an uneventful crossing.

Ten yards out it became deeper, with my own horse plunging down to his chest in the turbulent mass. There was only another twenty feet or so to the other bank and I was still holding onto Kate's hand when what must have been an uprooted tree struck violently into the side of her horse and she was knocked off his back. I was downstream of her as our hands tore loose from one another. She was gone in an instant.

I screamed her name as the roan finally found purchase on the gravel bed and began to pull us free of the water. Turning in the saddle, I saw proof of the fact that there is truly a benevolent God.

Miraculously, she had managed to seize hold of the tail of my horse in the moment of being swept away, and as the roan frantically sought the safety of the far bank, he pulled her clear of the violent water.

Of Kate's Arabian there was no sign. We never saw him again. I like to believe he got free of the surging stream farther down. However, most of our food, along with both of the rifles and spare ammunition, were lost.

I reached down to help Kate mount behind me on the roan. Her arms snaked around my chest in a tight embrace, and she nestled her ice-cold hands inside the pockets of my coat. Soaked and bedraggled, the two of us rode on toward Calvary.

Less than ten minutes later, we saw the first of the landmarks the man on the road had told us to look out for. At the clearing in the trees we turned off the road and followed a muddy lane until it ended in an ancient stand of hardwoods. To our left, the outline of a massive structure emerged through the wall of rain.

As we drew closer, a bolt of lightning enabled me to see that it ran at least four stories high and had what appeared to be medieval-style parapets in each corner. Much of it had been badly damaged by fire and the roof was missing from one entire wing. I could see gaping holes in the walls where there had once been windows.

We dismounted and walked stiffly toward the front entrance. The house was completely dark. I remember wondering what we would do if the major's friend was no longer there.

The door was iron-bound and looked stout enough to withstand a battering ram. A minute of loud knocking yielded no response. In desperation, I used the butt of my revolver to pound on the door, making a din that would have woken the dead.

Suddenly, Kate grabbed my arm and pointed to the glass-paneled transom over the door. I could now see a wavering light, which slowly grew stronger as someone approached it from the other side.

Still, whoever was there did not open the door. It was only when I began pounding again that we finally heard a key moving in the lock and it slowly swung open.

The figure of a man peered out at us. He was holding an oil

lamp in front of him and the force of the wind made the flame gutter wildly inside its glass chimney.

" 'Speak, thou apparition,' " he demanded in an odd, jolly-sounding voice.

There was a vacant cast to his face and for a moment I thought he might be blind. Then, birdlike, the restless eyes darted in my direction and looked me up and down.

He was a wiry little man, even shorter than me. A fringe of curly hair surrounded his bald skull and he had a sharp beak of a nose. When he spoke, he cocked his head to one side. All in all he reminded me of Chanticleer the rooster.

"Mr. Gamage?" I said.

" 'Unbidden guests are often welcomest when they are gone,' " he declared with an idiot's grin. I knew right away it was from Shakespeare but couldn't remember which play.

When I saw the door begin to shut on us, I said loudly, "Montague sent us."

Slowly, it swung open again. "Montague," he repeated. "Who perchance is Montague?"

"A man with one arm," I said.

"And so he is. And so he comes anon," said the man. With that he beckoned us in and closed the door behind us.

EIGHTEEN

IT WAS OBVIOUS the high-ceilinged front room was no longer in use. Aside from a brass chandelier with more arms on it than a sea serpent, all the furnishings had been removed. The dust on the floor was thick enough for us to make tracks in as we followed him through dark, empty corridors to the back of the great house.

We entered an immense kitchen, which was blessedly warm thanks to a black iron cookstove that took up most of one wall. A pile of stove wood was stacked to the ceiling right next to it. In the glow of lamplight, I could see a plantation table in the center of the room with ten chairs around it. Above it in the shadows was an iron rack from which hung a score of copper pots and cooking pans. The windows were all shuttered against the wind.

"Sit here next to the stove," he said with another vacuous smile. We gratefully did so.

"Are you hungry?" he asked.

"Yes," said Kate.

"Fine. We'll pluck a crow for you," he said, tittering with laughter. "But first I shall see to your horse."

The kitchen door was barred with a length of oak timber. He

removed the plank from its braces and opened it. Outside, the storm raged, unabated.

" 'Blow. Blow, thou winter wind! Thou art not so unkind as Man's ingratitude.' "

With that he slammed the door shut behind him and was gone.

"He's crazy, all right," I whispered.

"Without question he is a strange little man," said Kate, and I nodded agreement.

"But I don't believe he is crazy," she added.

"Why not?"

She gave me a sly smile and said, " 'I have no other but a woman's reason. I think him so because I think him so.' "

"The Taming of the Shrew?" I hazarded.

"Two Gentlemen from Verona," she responded, and we both laughed.

Then she said, "I believe he is playing a game with us and pretending to be unbalanced."

"Why would he do that?"

"For one thing it probably keeps strangers away," she said.

When I thought about it that made sense, although it didn't explain the mystery of who he was and what Major de Monfort had to do with him.

When the little man returned he went straight to a cold pantry off the kitchen and returned with a loaf of freshly baked bread and a whole baked chicken.

"Thank you, Mr. Gamage," I said, my mouth too full to be heard plainly.

" 'Tis an ill cook that cannot lick his own fingers," said Mr. Gamage, his restless eyes never still for a moment.

After our meal, he led us to our rooms on the second floor of the undamaged wing. The rooms adjoined one another and were connected by a common door. Unlike the rest of the house, they appeared to have been in recent use and were clean, with heavy goose-down comforters on each bed. The shutters on the windows were bolted shut from the outside and the windows covered by floor-to-ceiling drapes, which kept out any drafts from the raging wind.

There was even an abundance of candles and I soon had my room cheerily lit. A call from Kate in an excited voice brought me to a third chamber, smaller than the other two, in the middle of which there stood an enamel bathtub.

"The simplest and best of luxuries," she announced. "Mr. Gamage has promised to boil all the water we need if I'll carry it up."

"I don't need a bath," I said, although I knew I did. It was the thought of bathing around Kate that made me uncomfortable.

"Forgive me, Jamie, but you smell like a goat," she said. "I'll go first and then bring more hot water for you."

"Really. I got clean coming through the river," I persisted.

"Why, Jamie Lockhart, you're actually blushing," she said, putting her arm around me and grinning affectionately. "Now, I'm *not* inviting you to bathe with me."

Again, I felt the blood rushing to my face and turned away from her.

"For the Lord's sake, Jamie, I grew up with two older brothers."

An hour or so later, she had completed her ablutions and knocked on my door to tell me it was time for mine. When I let myself into the bath chamber, it was still full of steam. Apparently, she had found scented bath salts somewhere because the room smelled like it was full of honeysuckle.

Quickly stripping off my clothes, I stepped into the tub, cradling my burned hand along the edge of the rim. Then I let myself sink down until the water covered me right up to my neck. It was only then I truly appreciated why she had called it a luxury. As the heat began to soak into me, it was like a sooth-

ing balm to my aching muscles and joints. All the saddle soreness from a hundred miles of hard riding began to melt away.

Then the door sprang open and Kate stepped inside. She
was wearing a long red cotton robe, drawn tightly to her waist
with a matching belt. I knew she had nothing on underneath it.

"It is not too horrible, I hope," she said, coming over to
pick up my soiled clothes. She had washed her hair and it fell
in its wet fullness around her face as she leaned down to get my
things.

"No," I said.

"Mr. Gamage has offered to clean our clothes."

As she pushed her hair back away from her face, it was as if
I were just seeing her for the first time. I cannot tell you why,
but the way she looked right then has stayed in my mind ever
since. It wasn't any one thing over another—the green eyes like
brilliant stars or the pure ivory skin or the way her lips were
parted as she glanced back at me. But in that moment I knew I
loved Katharine Dandridge. As she went out of the room, I
could only stare after her in mute wonder.

While preparing for bed, we discussed the strange little man
and what his connection might be to Major Alain de Monfort.
I had no ideas on what it could be, although I remembered the
major telling me on that rainy night near New Market about the
orders which took him to the Yankee-held fortress at Winchester. Perhaps he was carrying out a secret mission behind the
lines. Maybe Mr. Gamage was part of it too. The best news was
that the major was coming to the house and might possibly be
free to accompany us on to Sudley Springs.

"Although our host definitely appears harmless," said Kate,
"it is better to be safe than sorry."

I watched as she carefully tucked one of her two pistols
under the pillows on her bed. I then did the same with mine.
We decided to lock the outer doors of our rooms but leave the
connecting door open.

Snuffing out the candles, I waited for my eyes to become accustomed to the darkness. Still wide awake after ten minutes, I found myself reeling with emotions and sensations I had never known before. A million thoughts raced through my mind at once, without the slightest clue of how to deal with any of them.

"Good night," I said, for the third time.

"Good night, Jamie," she called out softly from the other room.

I tried to think of something else to say. Something that would allow me to make my feelings plain and hear her voice just once more.

"I guess we've both read a lot of Shakespeare," I said lamely through the open door.

"Some," was the sleepy reply.

I summoned my courage and said with all the feeling I could give the words, " 'See! how she leans her cheek upon her hand: O! that I were a glove upon that hand, that I might touch that cheek.' "

Aside from the rain striking the shutters, there was complete silence for at least a full minute. Just when I thought she must have already fallen asleep, I heard her sweet, pure voice again.

" 'Here comes a strange beast which in all tongues is called a fool.' "

"As You Like It," I said morosely.

"Go to sleep," she ordered with mock severity, and I did.

NINETEEN

I awoke to the sight of a huge white rat sitting comfortably on the walnut table next to my bed. He was eating a piece of bread I had brought up with me after dinner, and clearly relishing every bite. I waited until he had finished before rustling the covers to attract his notice. He looked back at me with a stony gaze before deciding to take himself off to the corner where he disappeared behind a chest of drawers.

I went to the window and pulled back the drapes. It was shortly after sunrise and I could just see a sliver of sky through the bolted shutters. The storm had blown itself out during the night. Not only had the wind died to a whisper, but the skies were clear and blue for the first time in as long as I could remember.

Something caught my eye off in the trees that ringed the grounds around the house. As I watched, a man's form burst into view from the edge of the tree line. He ran without stopping until he disappeared off to the left in the general direction of the burned wing of the house.

"Kate," I called out urgently, as a second heavily bundled figure emerged from the trees and raced across the same open ground.

A moment later she was by my side. Even as I pointed to the spot where I had seen the first men come out, a third figure stepped from the tree line. Unlike the others, this one did not run. Rather, he scuttled along, dragging his left leg behind him. When he was halfway across the clearing, Kate rapped sharply on the window and the figure stopped in his tracks, staring upward in our direction. He could not see us because of the bolted shutters, but we could clearly see him.

He was a Negro man, coal-black. For a second he stood frozen in place. Then he dragged himself forward again until, like the others, he too disappeared off to the left.

"Runaways," murmured Kate.

"From where?"

"From all over the South," she said.

"He looked so scared."

"You would be too," she said. "If they're caught they are publicly flogged as an example to others. Or worse."

The third man was the last we saw. Afterward, I got dressed and went downstairs. Water was boiling on the stove but of Mr. Gamage there was no sign. He came in from outside as I was brewing a pot of tea for Kate. Barring it behind him, he took off his sheepskin coat and hung it on the peg next to the door.

"You have runaways hiding in the burned wing of this house," I said without inflection.

He cocked his head and, with the usual dullard's grin, replied, "Runaways?"

"Yes. Runaway slaves."

He pointed at me and said, " 'Not all those laid in bed majestical, can sleep so soundly as the wretched slave.' "

By this time I was roundly tired of his Shakespeare games and said with ill humor, "Can you please get word to Major de Monfort that we are here?"

"Who, pray tell, is that?" he said in his singsong cadence. "Major Alain de Monfort?"

He seemed genuinely puzzled.

"The one-armed man," I said in exasperation.

"Yes, I see, said the blind man. I see."

Going straight to one of the kitchen cupboards, he reached down for something on one of the lower shelves. When he stood up and turned around, he was holding a small pepperbox revolver.

His bird's eyes were no longer restless. They bored into mine. Indeed, his whole manner was different. The little man now looked very dangerous.

When he smiled again it was no longer a simpleton's act.

"Please be assured I still wish to provide you with every comfort," he said amiably. "Your pistol, for example. It looks exceedingly heavy and cumbersome. Let me relieve you of its burden."

With that, he stepped across the room and pulled it from my belt. Then he marched me upstairs. Kate had just finished dressing when he had me knock on the door to let us in. A quick but thorough search uncovered both of Kate's pistols.

"I do not yet know what to do with you," he said then. "I have no wish to harm you. In the meantime you will be forced to stay in here."

He locked each door in turn from the corridor and then we heard him retire down the stairs. Five minutes later, we heard footsteps coming back up again, followed by the sound of a chair being dragged into the hallway from another room down the hall. After that, it was quiet.

We were locked inside our rooms for the next two days. Mr. Gamage brought us our meals, and once each day a pitcher of water for washing. The only time he allowed us outside was to visit the privy, and that was one at a time. During those periods he covered us with his revolver until we were back under lock and key.

Apart from the fact that I was regaining limited use of my hand, there was only one thing to be said for it and that was being alone with Kate. Soon, however, she fell into a melancholy state and spent most of her time brooding at the possibility we would never catch up to her father's killers. I was grateful when Mr. Gamage brought two books along with our first evening meal.

One of them was a well-thumbed volume of Shakespeare that I assumed was his personal Bible. The second one introduced me to Charles Dickens. It is fair to say that reading the first half of *The Pickwick Papers* was just the tonic I needed then. Unfortunately, on those occasions when I could not contain my laughter, Kate would cast me a furious glance at the thought I could find any amusement in our current situation.

It was around midnight on the second night of our captivity, and Pickwick had just been imprisoned himself for breach of promise, when my eyes became so heavy the book collapsed on my chest and I must have dozed off.

I awoke to the sound of voices off in the same corner of my room where the white rat had disappeared. It could not have been long after I had fallen asleep because the candle next to my bed was still flickering and there was no sign of daylight coming through the shutters. At first the voices were muffled and indistinct. Then one of them was raised in anger.

I slipped out of bed and went over to the source of the sounds. They appeared to be coming from an iron mesh grate in the corner of the floor. Although I have never seen anything like it before or since, my guess is that it was designed to carry heat aloft from the rooms below. For sure they were not in the room directly below me or I would have heard them clearly.

One of the voices belonged to Mr. Gamage. The other seemed familiar but I could not place it at first. Then I realized it sounded like the major's voice, but somehow different. It was flat and tired, drained of spirit.

I still could not understand any of their words, and a short time later they removed to a place beyond my hearing. I crawled back into bed and pondered the mystery.

If it truly was Major de Monfort, why had he not come to us? Was it possible there was another man whose voice was similar to his? I wondered whether to waken Kate, but, of course, she had never met him. I finally fell back asleep with the thought that if it was him, we would learn something on the morrow.

On the third morning, we both arose a little after dawn, and were dismayed to discover in looking through the shutters that it was snowing again. When an hour passed with no sign of life from downstairs, we slowly became alarmed. Mr. Gamage had always come early in the morning to check on us.

I told Kate then about the angry voices I had heard in the night without mentioning I thought one of them might be the major. At first she thought I might have dreamed it, but as the morning wore on it became plain that something was indeed wrong. The air was becoming appreciably colder. Soon it became possible to see our breath in the air.

Finally, we decided to act. The brass hinge plates on my bedroom door were our first target but I found they were mortised too deeply into the frame for us to remove the pins. The doors themselves were made of solid oak and the keyed locks were anchored to the frame with iron bolts.

Our next effort was centered on the shuttered windows. The window frame itself presented no problem. It provided us with a three-foot opening when we raised the lower panel to its full extension. Our difficulty was with the shutters. The panels were held in place by two flat iron bars that fit into brackets on the outside wall. There was no way to reach them. The only way for us to escape was to batter a hole in the shutters themselves.

Standing on a chair, Kate removed the solid-mahogany curtain rod over the window frame. Using it like a battering ram, she began pounding on the bottommost wooden slat. It proved surprisingly tough to dislodge but we took turns at it and a minute later rammed it clear. In a short time, we had enlarged the hole to more than a foot. Now, the growl of the wind was more pronounced. It whirled a gust of snow into our faces through the opening we had made. We fell to the job again in earnest.

Suddenly, Kate said she thought she heard the sound of a horse out in the storm. I stopped pounding the shutter and waited. Sure enough, the horse renewed its trumpeting a moment later.

Not knowing who was coming, we stopped what we were doing and shut the window. Now wielding the heavy curtain rod as if it were a club, I positioned myself behind the hallway door.

The slam of the kitchen door flying open under the force of the wind was our first notice that someone was inside. Then we heard it being closed again.

Next, we heard the steps of someone coming up the stairs. He was climbing very slowly, as if each step were a challenge. I could hear the sound of labored breathing as his boots creaked down the hall. Then a key moved in the lock. I braced myself as the door swung slowly open.

From my position behind it, there was no way for me to see who it was. Kate was standing next to the bed, her startled eyes fixed on the person at the door.

"I am Alain . . . de Monfort," I heard him say in the strange familiar accent. By the time I stepped around the door, however, his eyes had already rolled up in his head and he was pitching forward into our arms.

TWENTY

HE LOOKED VERY different from our last meeting on the Valley Pike near New Market. Then, he had seemed unconquerable, like one of King Arthur's Knights of old.

Now, his slim bronze-colored body was gaunt, almost shrunken. The exposed skin of his face and hand appeared to be actually frozen, ice-cold and slick to the touch. It was while stripping off his gray, patched military cloak that Kate found the bullet hole in his side.

"He has lost a great deal of blood," she said as we dragged him to my bed.

When we raised him up so that Kate could remove his shirt, I saw for the first time the leather scabbard he wore strapped to his back. It still held the Louisiana toothpick he had used with lightning speed to kill Big Joe Braddock.

"See if you can find any spirits, Jamie," she ordered, while rubbing his arm in an attempt to restore circulation. "If there isn't a fire started, make one in the stove and put on some water."

I was already out the door when she called after me, "And find me scissors and clean material for a bandage."

As I raced down to the kitchen, I looked for any sign of Mr. Gamage but found none. The kitchen stove was ice-cold, although there was still split wood aplenty stacked against the wall. In a few minutes I had a good fire going, after which I put two copper pans full of water on to boil.

Searching the kitchen shelves, I uncorked a jug that definitely had "potency" and ran it back upstairs. The major was still unconscious, but Kate was able to force a few tablespoons of the liquor between his lips. After emitting a low groan, his eyes slowly parted and he took us in.

"Must leave here. Not safe," he murmured through gritted teeth.

Kate said, "You are in no condition to ride, Major."

"Have to. Can expect guests anytime now."

"In case you didn't notice, there is a blizzard out there," she said calmly. "Still—Jamie, find out if the roan is still in the barn. Also see if there is any kind of farm wagon."

I went out to the shed where Mr. Gamage had taken the roan on the night we arrived. He was standing placidly in a stall, munching hay. Sure enough, there was also an ancient buckboard in there, and although it had obviously seen many years of hard use, the wheels and axles looked solid and had been recently greased. I went and retrieved Major de Monfort's horse from the yard. Removing his saddle and bridle, I put him in another stall, pitching some hay in before rushing back to the kitchen.

By the time I returned to the room with the first large pan of hot water, he was talking freely.

"My brain may still be frozen, Miss Dandridge, but you have already melted my heart," he said with a small dash of his old spirit.

"You will have to do better than that, Major," she responded. "I am not one of your simpering New Orleans belles."

"They are but a fast-receding memory," he declared as she began to clean his wound. Turning to me, he said, "Now tell me everything that has happened since we parted."

It took some time to tell it all. When I came to what happened to Kate's father, I paused for a moment. With no apparent emotion, Kate said, "Do not worry about my feelings. Just tell him what happened, Jamie." And I did.

When I was finished, the major said, "You are both so brave as to be foolhardy. Are you still committed to going on?" We both nodded yes, and he shook his head in seeming wonder.

I said then, "Who shot you?"

He looked at me keenly and said, "I can only tell you it was fairly earned."

"Who is Mr. Gamage and what is he doing here?" I asked next.

"There will be time for questions later," interrupted Kate. "Help me with this."

Together, we propped him into a sitting position, which enabled me to see that the bullet had passed entirely through the side of his body. Kate covered both of the still-seeping wounds with folded layers of clean linen, before wrapping it tightly in place with longer strips of the same material. Aside from an involuntary grimace, the major did not complain. He only spoke when she attempted to remove the straps that held the leather scabbard in place for his Louisiana toothpick.

"I would ask you to leave my friend where he is," he said.

At no time during her ministrations did she appear to take notice of his missing right arm or the crudely amputated stump which was all that remained of it. After helping him into a clean woolen shirt, she turned to me again.

"We must make preparations to leave."

"To Sudley Springs?" I asked.

Before Kate could answer, the major said, "Yes. Sudley Springs."

"You will accompany us, Major?" said Kate with a thrill in her voice.

He nodded. "By the time we get there, Miss Dandridge, I should be able to help a bit with the men who killed your father . . . if they make it that far. In the meantime, I will try not to be a burden."

"Now we have a real chance against them," I said.

It was with renewed hope and excitement that we began loading the wagon. When I went searching for food in the pantry behind the kitchen, I was astonished to find baskets of onions, potatoes, and apples, along with smoked venison and other meats, including a great slab of bacon. There was even a small sack of salt. It was enough to convince me that Mr. Gamage had been a food hoarder. I took all that I could carry in two trips to the barn.

Kate had heated several bricks in the oven before bringing out all the goose-down comforters from the bedrooms. Placing the bricks inside the quilts, she made a warm bed for the major in the back of the wagon. In the space that was left, I loaded the food and what remained of the horse fodder in the barn.

While gathering together the harness trappings, I found an old canvas top for the wagon along with three flexible wooden struts that fitted into grooved slots along the sides. Working the struts into position, Kate and I stretched the canvas across them and strapped it down at the corners. It rose just two feet above the sides of the wagon but would provide some protection for him from the storm outside.

The next task was getting Major de Monfort from his bed
to the wagon. Propping him up between us, we maundered like
three drunken soldiers down the stairs and out into the snow.
When we finally got him into the bed of the wagon, Kate
wrapped him snugly inside the small mountain of comforters.

"Very cozy indeed," he said with a queasy but gallant smile.

We then set to the job of harnessing the two horses and
hitching them to the buckboard. The winter afternoon was already far advanced when at last we were ready to set out for Sudley Springs. The major had already given us a map he was
carrying that showed all the principal towns and roads along the
route we planned to follow. Kate and I went over it together for
several minutes until we felt sure of our bearings. When I went
to open the doors of the barn, the force of the wind actually tore
one of them off at the hinges. I climbed up next to Kate, who
snapped the reins several times on the horses' rumps in order to
coax them forward.

Given we had many gales in December, but none of them
prepared us for the blizzard that has since become widely known
as Lincoln's last Christmas present. Those of us who encoun-
tered its full fury will remember the experience for the rest of
our lives.

The snow was coming horizontally. It was already four
inches deep on the surface of the road and seemed to be falling
harder every minute. Kate rode head down, the brim of her
planter's hat partly shielding her face.

It was very hard going for the horses too, and they slipped
continually, trying to gain their footing on the icy track. I
watched as their tails froze into a solid mass. By then, the two
of us were coated in white from head to toe. Each time I began
to lose sensation in my feet, I would stamp them on the floor
of the buckboard until little needles of pain told me they were
all right again.

We saw only one other traveler on the road that whole day.

Head down, he came slowly out of the white wall ahead of us, a spectral phantom on horseback, going in the opposite direction. I don't think he ever saw us. In the event, we did not call out greetings to one another before he disappeared behind us.

As evening began to come down around us, the white world we were traveling in turned darker. There was no letup in the wind. At times it seemed strong enough to blow us right off the road, but the horses struggled on even as the snow mounted higher.

Every thirty minutes or so, I would climb into the back of the wagon to knock loose the snow that kept piling up on the canvas top and to see how Major de Monfort was faring. He slept through most of the journey, although once he looked up as I was leaning over him and I took the opportunity to say, "You were in Mr. Gamage's house the night before last. Why didn't you come for us?"

He was silent for a moment. Then, he said, "You're mistaken, Jamie."

"No I'm not. I heard your voice along with Mr. Gamage's."

"Do not pursue this," he said, turning away from me.

Now, I knew he was lying to me, but why? If he had been there the previous night then why had he gone off? And how had he gotten shot before coming back? I knew him to be a man of honor and could only believe there had to be a good reason for him to lie. If I could not place my faith in him after all he had done for me, then whom could I trust?

As I turned to go back to my seat next to Kate, he said, "I promise that you shall learn the truth in this matter when we reach Sudley Springs, Jamie."

After night fell, the road ahead of us became a solid gray mass. Except for the trees that bordered the track on both sides, it would have been impossible to know whether we were even still on the road. According to Major de Monfort's map, we should have long ago reached the settlement at Krick's Mill.

For more than an hour we had been traveling through what seemed like an endless stretch of woods, with snow-bent cedar and pine trees growing right to the edge of the road. Now, we came out into a succession of open windswept fields. It was here that the horses finally began to break down from their long valiant effort to pull the wagon forward. Feeling a sharp nudge from Kate, I turned to face her. Her mouth was moving but the words were lost in the fury of the tempest. I leaned closer.

"It's no good," she shouted. "I must have missed the Amissville road."

I saw despair in her eyes but it was at that same moment I also saw our salvation over her shoulder.

"Look there," I called out excitedly, pointing off toward the pasture on our left. On the far side of the open field I could see what looked like an implement shed. It was connected to an open lean-to that might once have sheltered livestock. The ancient hoary structure was canted over so far to one side, it appeared that one more gust of wind might well bring about its final collapse. Right then, however, it looked more inviting to me than my own homeplace.

With a strong pull on the reins, Kate turned the horses into the field and we crossed the pasture, pulling up under the lean-to as darkness finally settled around us.

TWENTY-ONE

THERE WAS A BRASS padlock on the door of the shed and I busted it open with one blow from the butt of the major's rifle. Then, Kate and I helped him inside. It was doubtful whether anyone had set foot in the place for years. The shack was filled with sprung barrels, crocks, decayed leather tack, and an assortment of mostly broken farm tools. One corner of the roof was missing and snow had piled up a foot high in that corner.

The most important discovery was a gigantic cast-iron butcher kettle that stood on three legs. The major immediately saw its possibilities as a stove and had me drag it under the open section of the roof. At his direction, I used the head of a broken pickax to punch three small holes in its rusted bottom. Starting with a few handfuls of wood shavings, I soon built a steady fire using the sprung barrel staves. As the iron heated, it began to throw off a warmth that was very welcome against the savage wind that gusted through the cracks in the walls.

Going back outside, Kate and I unharnessed the horses and

put them in the one sheltered corner of the lean-to. After giving them a good rubdown, I left sufficient fodder for the brutal night ahead. We then unpacked the wagon, bringing in the comforters and all of the food supplies.

Major de Monfort had already plugged the larger cracks in the walls using old rags, and it was becoming almost cheery inside, with the intense little fire turning the sides of the kettle a dull red.

After warming her hands for a few minutes, Kate startled both of us by declaring that she planned to cook us all a hot meal. This alchemy was made a little easier by another invention of the major's. He had me make it for her out of metal barrel hoops that I flattened with my boot. Then, he showed me how to join them together in a crisscross fashion. When I laid the meshed iron strips across the rim of the butcher pot, it made a perfect cooking surface.

She made our first supper in a deep skillet pan we had brought with us in the buckboard. It was hot corn porridge, flavored with apple chunks and molasses. This may not sound appetizing now, but at the time it tasted awfully good. Just the flavorful smell of it bubbling in the skillet reminded me of how long it had been since I had eaten anything at all. By then, there was only a constant gnawing inside me, as if my stomach were feeding on itself. An hour later, it was no longer complaining.

The snow kept coming as if it would never stop. Among the three of us, we kept the animals fed and one of us kept stoking the fire with more barrel staves and short sections of the floor joists. I'm not sure how cold it actually got that first night, although I have seen a newspaper account since in which a man from Coote's Store claims he recorded a temperature of nineteen degrees below zero. I do know this. When I accidentally spilled a ladle of water on the floor, it glazed right into ice before our eyes.

As dawn broke, I went to the window and scraped away the frost web that covered it like new skin. Looking out, I beheld a scene of wonder. Everything within view was buried under a several-foot-thick blanket of white. The branches of the trees were no longer even recognizable under the weight of their burden. Nothing moved in that barren landscape save the snow and the endless wind.

The blizzard kept its strength through much of the next day. It was impossible to know for sure when it actually stopped because the wind blew so crazily that at times it appeared the snow was actually falling upward. When it did finally end, the wind had swirled it into drifts that in some places grew to eight feet or more. One of them completely buried the eastern wall of the shack.

There was no choice but to try to be patient. We could go nowhere until the snow receded. Aside from going out to check the horses, we just tended the fire and tried to keep occupied.

The major busied himself with his weapons. Bracing his "toothpick" between the floor and a table leg, he proceeded to sharpen both edges of the blade with a whetstone. It took him almost half an hour, but after he was finished, the blade was razor-sharp. When I made the mistake of testing the tip of it, the point actually punctured my finger.

Then the major disassembled his revolver, methodically cleaning each part with an oil-soaked rag. It was amazing what he could do with just the fingers of his left hand. After putting it together again, he examined each of the loads before inserting them back into the chambers. Then, he showed me how to clean his Sharps rifle.

As the major regained his strength, he also became more spirited. After our evening meal, he spent an hour entertaining us with vivid stories of life before the war in Louisiana's Bayou

La Frenière. With an almost unseemly eagerness, Kate begged to hear more, and he proceeded to talk for a long while about the colorful people of the Attakapas and their fascinating ways. The years seemed to melt away from him, and as I watched his black eyes dancing in the firelight, I could see how handsome he must have been in his younger days before the war.

After that, he and Kate began to converse in French, the language which he spoke as almost a native tongue, and for which she had acquired a fair knowledge in school. They engaged in a lengthy discourse, which, of course, I did not understand. To my keen disappointment, neither one of them made any attempt to enlighten me. At one point, they both laughed heartily at some amusing episode and it was all I could do to contain my anger. By then, she was calling him Alain. He stayed with the more formal Katharine.

I know the major was just being his gallant self, but as the hours passed, I found myself taking an active dislike to his manner, especially toward Kate. And I must say that she too seemed a different person than the girl I thought I had come to know. On the rare occasions when I found the major turning to look at me, I would catch her giving him sidelong glances that were very unbecoming considering the difference in their ages. They were still talking in French when I burrowed under my comforters and went to sleep.

The next morning I awoke to find Kate lying by my side, her thick auburn hair all that was visible above the covers. The major appeared to be asleep in the other corner with his head resting on one of the horses' breast collars. However, when I moved to get up, his eyes opened immediately, focused and alert. Then, they relaxed and he smiled at me.

All my joints felt cramped and stiff. Going to the water bucket, I cracked the surface ice and washed my face. Buttoning my coat, I went outside to strip some more wood from the lean-to. It seemed a little warmer that day, although I couldn't be sure. Back inside, I quietly stoked the fire back up. As I was changing into my last pair of clean socks, Kate stirred awake beside me. Her beautiful green eyes came alive as she took us both in.

"Joyeux Noël, mes amis," she said with a radiant smile.

"Et à vous aussi, Katharine," said the major. "Happy Christmas, Jamie."

That was how I discovered what day it was, and a wave of sadness came over me then. It was the first one I had ever spent away from home, and at that moment I would have given Stonewall Jackson's gold to be in my own bed, waiting with anticipation for my parents to say it was all right to come to the tree. Kate must have seen the sadness in my eyes.

"What would my heroes like for their Christmas dinner?" she said.

"Crawfish en croûte and a roast of beef, *très saignant,*" said the major with only a hint of a smile. "For dessert, raspberries in clotted cream."

"Je regrette, Alain," she said. "And you, my young knight?"

"Fatback and beans," I said, and she laughed.

"A man after my own heart under the circumstances," she said, "but I think I can do a little better than that."

She did far better than that. Later that morning, as the wind continued to whistle and moan outside our snowbound refuge, I watched Kate prepare our Christmas meal.

In the deep skillet she placed a slab of bacon, which right away began to spit and crackle in the heat of the fire. Then, she began slicing onions into the oil, four in all. As soon as that heavenly aroma reached my nose, I impatiently began to wonder how long it would take before it was finished. Next came little red potatoes and a huge turnip, followed by two gnarly carrots and chunks of venison and rabbit.

I watched as she stirred the pot with one hand while pushing her hair out of her eyes with the other. Several times, she thinned the mixture with melted snow. Later, she added a generous dose of the liquor we had used to arouse the major after he fainted back at the house.

While the savory stew bubbled in the deep skillet, Major de Monfort suggested I attempt to reconstruct Lieutenant Shawnessy's map from memory and I agreed to try. Kate handed me a charcoal pencil along with Johnny Bellayne's notebook. I turned to a blank page.

After staring at it for several minutes I finally shook my head.

"It's no use," I said. "Parts of it are there but I can't make it come back whole."

"That's all right," said Major de Monfort. "Just put down the things you can recollect."

I followed his advice and began to fill in the page. At first, I could only remember the intersecting lines and the little box with the cross in it that Dr. Cassidy had said was the Sudley Springs church. As I worked, other details began to come back and I penciled them in where I thought they belonged. The last thing I could remember was where the black half circle fit, along with the words "Mouth of the Devil."

That was it. As hard as I tried to force my mind to recover the other numbers and markings, the only thing I was able to achieve at that point was a throbbing headache.

My frustration must have showed plainly because that was when Kate said, "Don't worry about it now, Jamie. Put the notebook aside. It is time for our Christmas feast."

I was so grateful to her for that. It was as if she had removed a great weight from my shoulders. And what a feast it was.

I wasn't listening very closely but I believe the major told us that where he came from it was called ragoo. To me it just looked like a great meaty stew ladled in huge portions over steaming cornmeal cakes. I had my fill of the soft delicious chunks of meat in the rich broth, after which the major had us toast the holiday with more of the spirits from the stone jug.

I felt truly content and was beginning to nod off again when Major de Monfort said, "Jamie, I want to attempt a little experiment. Would you be willing to help me?"

"Of course," I replied, yawning.

"I just want you to lie down. Make yourself as comfortable as you can."

I lay back under my quilt and turned to face him.

"Good. Now I want you to close your eyes," said the major. "Close your eyes and just try to slow your mind down. Try not to think of anything at all."

I followed his instructions.

"Is your mind clear?" I heard him ask from what seemed far away.

"I'm falling asleep," I mumbled, at which Kate burst out laughing.

"All right, Jamie. Now I want you to think back to the day when you first showed the map to Dr. Cassidy. Do you remember that day?"

"Yes."

"Bon," he said. "Now in your mind's eye, I want you to go back to that very moment when the doctor first looked at the map with you. Are you there?"

"Yes, I am," I replied honestly. In my mind's eye I was already transported back to the doctor's walnut-paneled office, surrounded by all his books. For just a second I thought I could actually smell the whiskey on his breath as we stared down at the map together.

"Do you see it, Jamie? Can you see it now?" he asked quietly.

Amazingly, I did. It was all there in front of me, every detail on the dead man's map.

Hurriedly, I opened my eyes and began to transfer the image onto paper, worried that it would disappear again. At first, I just tried to make sure I got the letters and numbers right. After that I worked on getting the proportions as close as possible to what I saw in my mind. Finally, I put the pencil down and closed my eyes again, bringing the map alive in my brain one last time. Opening them, I looked at the paper. The images were as close to identical as I could make them. I handed the map to Major de Monfort. It is reproduced here.

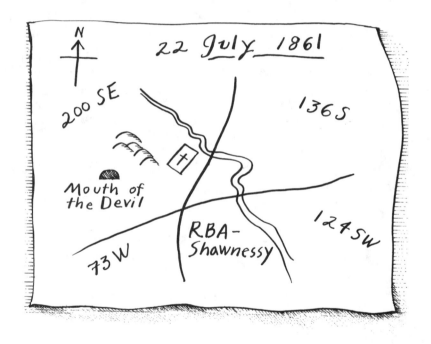

"Congratulations," he said with a smile as Kate actually came over and hugged me. Then the two of them began to examine it from every angle. It was the major who spoke first.

"I believe the starting point for this quest is the Sudley Springs church," he said.

"Why is that?" I asked. Kate answered the question for him.

"It is the only fixed landmark on the map, Jamie," she said. "Everything else—the streams, the roads—have no point of reference."

"Agreed," said the major as he continued to turn it in every direction.

"Then there are these other markings, 200SE, 136S, 124SW, and 73W," he went on. "Since they are scrawled on each corner of the map, it is impossible to know their proper order. Obviously, they include points on a compass. The numbers—"

"Must be distances," said Kate.

"Paces?" I suggested.

"Probably, Jamie," said Major de Monfort.

"Or possibly rods," said Kate. "If Lieutenant Shawnessy was from Ireland, he might have calculated distances with other measurements. Leagues and so forth."

"We'll have a better chance of discovering that answer once we have seen the ground, Katharine," said the major. "Then we can try out different formulas if necessary."

"What about the Mouth of the Devil?" I asked.

"That is clearly the hiding place our late lieutenant chose for the gold," said Kate.

Going to our diminishing wood supply, I placed part of a wet locust beam from the lean-to in the fire. It spit and hissed before bursting into flame.

"Let us speak of the Devil," said the major with a sardonic grin. "Satan, Lucifer, and Beelzebub."

"Gog and Magog," I added.

"The Angel of the Bottomless Pit," said Kate.

"And where is the Devil to be found?" he asked.

"The netherworld," said Kate. "In *The Divine Comedy*, Dante portrayed Hell in the lower regions. I would guess the gold is underground."

In my mind's eye I saw Lieutenant Shawnessy, carrying the heavily weighted crates in his powerful arms. What possible hiding place could he have found in the darkness and confusion of that long-ago night? Then it came to me.

"A well," I exclaimed. "He dropped the crates down a well . . . deep under the earth."

"You may be proven right, Jamie, but I don't think so," said the major, again staring at the map.

"Why not?" I challenged him. At the time I thought he was just trying to deny me the credit for finding the solution to the mystery.

"Two reasons. First, the Devil resides in a place of eternal fire. The bottom of a well is dark but wet. For the second reason just look at this," he said, pointing at the large black half circle next to the words "Mouth of the Devil."

"If he hid the gold in a well, then why not a full circle?"

That was the end of our speculations for the evening. It was after dark by then and Kate suggested we sing our favorite Christmas carols together. For all of his manly courage, the major demurred, pleading that his voice had suffered mightily from four years of sleeping on the ground. My own excuse consisted of turning red in the face.

So Kate sang alone, and I am forever grateful she did. Her voice was sweet and pure, and she needed no accompaniment as she sang "The First Noel." Both the major and I looked on with open admiration.

"Très belle, très belle, Katharine," said the major when she was finished.

"Merci, Alain," she replied with a self-conscious smile.

She then sang "God Rest Ye Merry Gentlemen," "Angels We Have Heard on High," and finally, "Hark! The Herald Angels Sing."

When she completed the last hymn, I can only say that it left me more in love with her than I could ever hope to express. A few minutes later, Major de Monfort went out to check the horses. I was staring into the fire and lost in my reverie when I heard her say, "Merry Christmas, Jamie."

I looked up to see her kneeling at my side and holding out a lace-trimmed handkerchief. It was tied into a pouch with a green hair ribbon.

"What is it?" I asked.

"It is my Christmas present to you," she said.

I was immediately overcome with guilt at having nothing to give her in return.

"I don't . . . I forgot—" I began, but she gently put her fingers to my lips.

"This is of small import for saving my life," she said. "May it keep you safe from harm."

I opened the handkerchief. Inside was a small gold cross affixed to a thin gold chain.

"My father gave it to me on my fourteenth birthday," she said. "I have worn it ever since."

"I can't . . ." I started to say, but she was already placing it around my neck and connecting the tiny clasp.

"Merry Christmas," she said again and then kissed me warmly on the cheek.

I was still feeling the imprint of her lips when the door of the shed flew open and Major de Monfort stepped back inside. If he noticed anything unusual in my manner, he was too much of a gentleman to comment on it.

When we awoke on the day after Christmas, it was to another of the Lord's manifest wonders. The sun was shining brightly and the snow on the trees was disappearing in front of our eyes. What I had thought was rain was actually a steady stream of melting snow pouring off the edge of the roof. The sudden rise in temperature was providential. By then, we had burned all the barrel staves in the shack as well as most of the lean-to's side walls and support posts.

As we waited in anticipation for the moment we could leave, the major outlined his plans for our arrival in Sudley Springs. The first thing to be done, he said, was to search for the gold. At this, Kate appeared to be taken aback. The major explained his reasoning this way.

If we went after McQuade and his gang first, there would be no time to search for the gold later, regardless of the outcome of our confrontation. If, for example, we captured some of the gang alive, he pointed out we would have no means of guarding them while we looked for the gold. And, if there was a pitched gun battle, which he considered the far more likely prospect, the Yankees would be down on us so quickly we would have to escape south before having any chance to find it.

I said I agreed with his thinking.

The next feature of his plan was to go in at night. He thought this gave us a far better chance of eluding them while we searched for the gold. As he went on to discuss his plans for muffling the noise from the wagon, I could see Kate was becoming more agitated. I knew she cared not one whit about the gold. Her sole purpose in being there was to track down the men who killed her loved ones.

As if divining her thoughts, the major turned to her and said, "Once we have the gold, Katharine, you have my pledge that I will go after your father's killers."

She stared at him keenly for a few seconds, and finally nodded her agreement. The major then showed us how to make crude tallow dip lanterns out of some empty fruit tins. At his direction, I used my clasp knife to cut a small window in each one of them. He said the lanterns would allow us to search for the gold at night. In the event of danger, we could cover the opening with our hands and cut off all light.

That was the last day we were marooned. This will probably sound crazy, but as the snow retreated and the time came closer to make the last part of our journey to Sudley Springs, I began to feel almost sorry to leave. It's strange how a place where you are stormbound can all of a sudden start feeling like home. Maybe it was because we had all come through the tempest safely. I don't know.

TWENTY-TWO

 EARLY THE NEXT MORNING
we left for Sudley Springs.
The major seemed almost
fully recovered from the
wound in his side, although
when Kate changed his
dressing for the last time,
the entry wound was still leaking blood.

He now rode up front in the wagon next to Kate, his Colt
revolver under the blanket on his lap. As Kate had surmised at
the height of the blizzard, we had missed our turnoff to
Amissville. It was necessary to retrace our path almost a mile to
pick up the Amissville road.

One lane had already been cleared by a horse-drawn plough
and it was much easier going for the horses. Snow still blanketed
the entire landscape but in the warmth of the sparkling sun it
had already shrunk to less than a foot in most places.

We passed through Ben Venue, and then Amissville. Everywhere we looked, people were coming out of their forced hi-
bernation like hungry bears, furiously shoveling snow from their
porches and stoops and clearing paths to their barn or to the
road. People were even walking along the roads again and the
paths were quickly turned into small seas of mud and slush.

We were just on the other side of Amissville when Major de
Monfort suddenly exclaimed, "Quel nigaud! He was in the
Pittsburgh wagon."

"Who?" said Kate and I at exactly the same time.

"Lieutenant Shawnessy," he replied with excitement. "Jamie, show me the map again."

I retrieved it from my pocket and opened it for him.

"See these distance points? The ones marked 200SE, 136S, 73W, and 124SW?"

"Yes," we said again at the same time.

"It makes it so much easier for us." I was glad he thought so but his point was still a riddle to me.

"By all accounts, Lieutenant Shawnessy was a very powerful man," he went on. "But even he could not have carried three crates of gold all those distances. So he must have remained in his wagon."

"Which means," said Kate, "that if he was in the wagon while he searched for a hiding place, then we can assume those compass headings have to follow roads or wide paths his wagon team could have traveled."

"Exactly," said Major de Monfort.

"Why could he not have left the wagon at the church and found the hiding place on foot?" I asked.

"There was not time, Jamie. Remember what Captain McQuade told you? When he returned to camp, Shawnessy was already there waiting for him."

"Alain's right," said Kate, and I had to agree.

"How would Lieutenant Shawnessy have known exactly how far he had gone in each direction?" I asked.

"He was probably walking the horses very slowly and counting the paces off in his head as he went," said the major.

Each step of our own horses took us farther into Yankee-controlled territory, but the major seemed oblivious to the danger. Then again, the sight of a one-armed man, a woman, and a boy might not have seemed all that threatening to Grant's army. We crossed the Hegeman River near Carter's Mountain, and at noon reached Warrenton. I felt a thrill knowing we were now no more than twenty miles from learning the secret of Lieutenant Shawnessy's map.

Since the major thought McQuade might have sent one of his gang to watch for us at Thoroughfare Gap, we crossed the southern flank of the Bull Run Mountains at New Baltimore, stopping to water the horses along another angry and swollen stream just to the west of Gainesville.

It was from those foothills above New Baltimore that I saw the end of the war. It was in the form of a huge military camp that lay spread out like a city as far as we could see toward Gainesville. There must have been a thousand tents, each one large enough to house a dozen soldiers. And just like buildings in a city, they were laid out in precise rows, with exactly the same amount of space between each one, and divided by macadamized streets large enough for two wagons to pass.

The major said it was just one of the many support camps for Union reserve troops who were supporting Grant's final thrust toward Petersburg. In that moment I realized my father and the rest of Lee's little army were doomed. If Mr. Lincoln could afford to keep ten thousand men in shiny new uniforms sitting so far away from the field of battle, then there was truly no hope for the Southern cause. Perhaps the gold could be used to help the men in that soon-to-be-defeated army rebuild their lives and homes, I concluded.

At the major's direction Kate circled south away from the encampment, only later coming back in an easterly direction on a lane that brought us to the other side of Gainesville. There was a lot more traffic on the road now. It consisted mainly of sutlers carrying their wares to and from the camp we had just passed.

A mile or so beyond Gainesville, something curious happened. We were passing a succession of seedy establishments that obviously served the military trade when the major asked Kate to halt the wagon. Off to the left and set back a little ways from the highway, there was a decrepit, flat-roofed log shanty. It looked like the kind of place that sold fruits and vegetables in the summer. A Negro man dressed in rags was seated on a log bench under its overhanging roof.

The major stared at the place for a moment and then slipped his Colt revolver inside the belt of his breeches. Swinging out from his seat, he dropped to the ground, sinking in the slush and mud up to his ankles before working his way to firmer ground.

"What is it?" asked Kate.

"We need tallow for the lanterns," he said.

When he reached the front of the store, he looked neither right nor left before entering. As he disappeared through the leather curtains that sufficed for a door, the Negro man got up from his bench and followed him inside.

Ten minutes passed by and still he did not reappear.

"I don't like this at all," said Kate.

The Sharps rifle lay next to her, its barrel resting on the seat.

"What should we do?" I asked.

"If he is not back soon, I'm going in there," she said, placing the rifle in her lap.

Less than a minute later, the leather curtains parted and the major strode out alone, carrying a small clay pot in his left hand. Before climbing back in the buckboard, he handed it up to me. Sure enough, it contained a large greasy chunk of tallow, sufficient to keep our lanterns well supplied through a long night's search.

"What took you so long?" Kate asked in a tone that revealed her concern.

"The storekeeper had to send his boy for it," he said.

Late that same afternoon, we came to the last leg of our journey, arriving at the far edge of the great battlefield at Manassas. It was here that the Northern and Southern armies had collided twice over the course of the war. I felt a thrill, knowing we might be following the same path my father once trod, since he had fought there both times.

Light was fading from the sky as we came in from the west on a logger's road that roughly paralleled the Warrenton Turnpike. Off to our left was a stony ridge and to the right were a succession of open snow-spattered fields. We only had to look at the trees to know what terrible destruction had been wrought there.

Many of the biggest trees were splintered as if by giants playing with axes. Others had been entirely shaved of their bark. One complete line of smaller trees had been cut off at the height of a man's heart.

It was at this point we came to a wide ditch in the ground that seemed to angle off to the northeast for as far as I could see. It was about twenty feet wide and more than three feet deep. Obviously, a great number of men had worked for a long time to construct it, but for what purpose I had no idea. The major appeared to know exactly where we were and said it was only a mile from there to Sudley Springs. We turned off the logger's road and followed the cut in the ground as it passed through several more stands of woods.

I began to see evidence that many men had fought along this line in one or both of the battles. There was wreckage and debris strewn along the embankment, including shattered caissons, broken musket barrels, ammunition boxes, and the large rib bones of what I assumed to be horses and mules. In some places logs had been laid end to end along the top of the cut. Each of them bore dozens of bullet scars.

Melted snow was running off the stony ridge and pouring down in a torrent across the fields. One of the streams ran straight through a makeshift cemetery where hundreds of stakes marked the locations under which dead soldiers still lay. In the years since the battle, most of the stakes had been uprooted by the elements. They were scattered everywhere on the ground.

In seeing this, my first thought was of families like mine that would never learn the final resting place of their husband or father. But then I saw something far worse. At one point, the stream had completely washed away the surface of the soil in its path. Near one of the grave markers, two scavenging dogs were fighting over something still half-buried in the ground. I quickly turned away.

Major de Monfort had Kate halt the wagon in a heavy copse of trees. She and I unharnessed the horses and hobbled them in a small clearing, spreading out enough fodder to last them the night. While we waited for full darkness, the major produced a brass-plated compass, which he experimented with in a long circuit around our campsite. I filled our handmade lanterns with tallow. Although Kate and I said we weren't hungry, the major made us eat something to give us strength for the long night ahead.

An hour later, we set out on foot for the Sudley Springs church.

TWENTY-THREE

IT WAS A CLEAR windy night, with huge billowy clouds racing across the dark starry sky in a silent armada. In the distance I could hear the lonely wail of a train whistle. We moved in single file, with the major in the lead, and me in the rear. He carried a lantern in his hand. The compass hung from a leather strap around his neck. The Colt revolver was under his cloak. Kate carried the Sharps rifle over one shoulder and a lantern in her other hand. I had both a lantern and a long-handled spade.

The ground was soft and we made no noise as we walked. Every hundred yards or so, Major de Monfort stopped to check the compass and adjust his bearings. As much as possible, we stayed off roads, moving through tree stands wherever we found them along our route. He only allowed us to cross an open space after scouting ahead himself to make sure the ground was safe. In this way, we came to Sudley Springs church without incident.

It was a large brick structure with three tall windows along each side in the middle of a patch of mostly cleared ground. From what I could see, the building was unmarked by the battles that had been fought around it, although most of the glass in the windows was cracked or missing.

Although three different roads intersected near the building, Kate and the major had both agreed the starting point for our search should be the front entrance to the building where it met the road. That was where we now stood.

Major de Monfort checked the compass heading of the road in front of the church, which turned out to be southwest. There was only one southwest heading from among the four clues on the map. It read 124SW. Accordingly, we began walking in that direction, each of us silently counting our paces as we went. The road remained straight and true. When I was on my one hundred and twenty-third pace, the major whispered, "Here," and Kate nodded her agreement.

I felt a surge of excitement as my lantern revealed we were standing at the intersection of another road. There were now only three compass headings left to choose from . . . 200SE, 136S, and 73W.

The major checked the compass heading of the new road.

"Due west," he said softly.

It appeared to be a logger's path, with old stumps lining the passage on both sides. Nevertheless, it was definitely wide enough for a wagon to pass through. I don't know about the others, but right then I was convinced the mystery was solved and had already begun thinking about how we would bring the gold away.

Several paces farther along, we came up against a solid wall of trees. At that point I had only counted forty-two steps. Something was obviously wrong. It should have been seventy-three. Using his lantern, the major and Kate examined the map again, finally shaking their heads in confusion.

"The only thing we can do is start again at the beginning," he whispered.

We made our way silently back to the church and stopped again at the front entrance. Since the first road was the only one to run in a southwesterly direction, the next possibility was to examine whether Lieutenant Shawnessy might have started from one of the other two.

One of them ran from north to south. It was the next one we explored. Unfortunately, as we walked south away from the church, the road began to veer sharply east and when we reached the ascribed distance of one hundred and thirty-six paces, there was no break to be found between the trees that was large enough for a wagon to pass by. We continued the search for another twenty paces with no success before turning back.

By this time, almost four hours had passed since we had left camp. Although the distances revealed in the clues were not in themselves very far, the major would stop at every noise and wait until it could be identified. He refused to take the slightest chance we might alert one of McQuade's gang to our presence. Once, the distant sound of a man on horseback kept us motionless for an hour while he went off to investigate.

Back at the church, Major de Monfort took a sighting on the one remaining road. This one ran roughly east to west, which corresponded with the marking 73W. Seventy-three paces later, we thought we might finally be in luck. We were at the edge of an open pasture that ranged still farther to the south. All three of the remaining compass headings led south and there was no reason to believe Lieutenant Shawnessy might not have chosen this open field rather than a road to find his eventual hiding place for the gold.

Over the next few hours we tried each one of the other headings in turn. The first two proved to be almost immediate failures, but the third one, 200SE, actually came out near a road with another southerly heading. This caused renewed hope, but when we finally arrived at the conclusion of our passage, all we found was another stand of dense woods. Fruitlessly, we searched among the trees for anything that could possibly be the Mouth of the Devil.

By then, we were all cold and footsore. It was past three

o'clock in the morning. Defeated, the major and Kate decided to abandon the search for that night and return to camp.

Dark clouds had again blotted out the stars and I could smell more rain in the air as we slowly made our way back across the vast battlefield. I have never believed in ghosts but can truthfully say it was very eerie to cross that ground in the dead of night. Listening to the dreadful moan of the wind, I began to imagine it was the departed souls of the thousands of Yankees and Confederates who had died there that were now joined together in making that sad refrain.

When we arrived back at our camp near the deep cut, all of us were too tired to discuss what had gone wrong in our search. As usual, the major volunteered to stand guard on the first watch. It started to drizzle as I wearily climbed into the back of the wagon and crawled under the covers. An instant later, I was dead asleep.

TWENTY-FOUR

IT RAINED STEADILY all the next day. Mostly, we stayed in the wagon, watching the water drip off the edges of the canvas top and splash into the small lake that grew around us. Meanwhile, we talked about the reasons for our failure the night before.

After hours of discussing each possible mistake, Kate said, "Jamie, are you absolutely sure you remembered everything from the map?"

I closed my eyes then and concentrated on bringing it back in my mind. Again, it was all there, just as I saw it that night in the rain at New Market before going over the mountain.

"Yes. I'm positive it's complete," I said, after opening my eyes and looking at the map in my hand.

"Then that means the lieutenant deliberately left something out that we need to know, Alain," said Kate.

"He may have wanted to give himself some additional security," agreed Major de Monfort.

"I believe it has to be the number of paces," I said. "What if after counting them out in his head each time, he just cut the number in half before writing it down?"

"Or added a certain number of paces to each of the numbers," said Kate.

"That is too easy," said the major. "Shawnessy was an intelligent man . . . and very careful too."

"Yes he was," agreed Kate, "but as you have already pointed out, Alain, he had very little time. He was already back at camp when McQuade returned with the others."

"Perhaps you're right," he said, pausing again to examine the map. "Well, I'm still convinced the road in front of the church is the one he must have started out from. Tonight, we will begin from there and simply double each of the distance numbers on the map just as Jamie has suggested. Since the direction of the road is southwest, we will walk two hundred and forty-eight paces and see what we find."

Several hours later we were back at the front entrance of the church and ready to test the new theory. What we found after walking off the specified distance was another road with a westerly bearing in exactly the right place. One hundred and forty-six paces after that, we found a wide lane, this one heading due south. Again doubling the number of paces, we arrived at what we hoped would be the last piece of the puzzle.

I could not help myself from running ahead as we neared the requisite number of steps. Unmasking my lantern, I almost shouted with joy as I beheld another road in precisely the right place. The major quickly checked his compass and discovered it ran southeast, just as it should have.

The last four hundred paces brought us to a small country

crossroads. If we were correct, the Mouth of the Devil had to be somewhere close to the place we were now standing. Unmasking our lanterns again, we could see the shadowy outlines of deserted structures on all four corners of the intersecting roads.

As we drew closer, it became obvious there had been fierce fighting here in at least one of the Manassas battles. The first building was burned to the ground, and the one directly across the road had taken a direct hit from cannon fire. It was in ruins.

We started our search in the other two, which were still intact. They were both small, one-room log cabins. The first was missing its front door and we just walked inside. Anything of value had long since been taken away or looted. All that was left was a sprung horsehair sofa in one corner and a few shattered sticks of furniture strewn across the floor. Otherwise, it was empty.

The second was equally bare except for a terrified groundhog who had taken up residence near the window we used to gain entrance. He tore madly around the room until Kate opened the door and he escaped into the night. A quick search uncovered nothing that resembled a black half circle or brought to mind the "Mouth of the Devil."

The major had stayed outside searching the grounds and joined us when we finished looking through the cabins.

"There are no wells that I can find, Jamie," he said in response to my earliest guess about the lieutenant's hiding place. "The people must have drawn water from the stream that runs behind there," he said, pointing at the building that had absorbed the direct hit.

It was the last place left to explore, and I walked toward it with a sinking heart. If there was nothing to be found in or around it, then our search would again have ended in failure.

This building was much larger than the others, and had been constructed of red brick. Three of the walls were still left standing, although part of the roof had collapsed and every window was blown out. While Kate waited by the door with the Sharps rifle, the major and I stepped through one of the empty window frames.

There was rubble everywhere and it was difficult to move about. Aside from shattered bricks, plaster, and broken glass, most of what littered the floor appeared to be farm tools and metal implements. A giant anvil lay upside down next to an iron plough. Nearby, there must have been a half-dozen shovel heads, along with an equal number of double-edged ax blades and a raft of long-toothed pitchforks.

"It must have been a place that sold farm implements," I whispered.

"Perhaps," said the major. Then, lifting his lantern high above his head, he asked, "What do you think this is?"

The object was so strange and monstrous in aspect that I momentarily drew back in awe. Cloaked in shadow, it first appeared to be the leather hide of some enormous beast with its tail hanging down toward the floor.

As I continued to stare at it, I saw the thing was made of sewn-together leather skins, connected by two huge panels of wood. What I first thought was a tail proved in reality to be nothing more than a long leather strap. While I watched, the major put down his lantern and pulled on the strap. One of the wooden panels drew close to the other, and it emitted a loud wheezing sigh.

"It is a bellows, Jamie," said the major. "The biggest one I have ever seen."

"What is it doing here?" I asked.

"If I am not mistaken, this place was a foundry," he said, moving farther into the shadowy interior.

"Then this must have been the forge," I said, holding my lantern in front of me as I stepped over the fallen debris. In the center of the room I now beheld two massive walls of brick, which as they rose higher, converged with two more interior walls toward what must have been a chimney. The major had already disappeared into the darkness when I turned the corner of the interior wall.

"And here is the Mouth of the Devil," I said quietly.

Actually, it looked more like a serpent's maw. The opening in the forge started several feet above the floor and ran horizontally for another six. Above it, the charred brickwork was arched into a half circle that receded into a fire pit where the metal was once heated and wrought.

The major came around the corner and stopped short.

"By all that is holy, Jamie, I believe you have found it," he whispered.

The opening was almost a perfect half circle. It had to be where Lieutenant Shawnessy had hidden the gold, but there was only one way to find out for sure. Major de Monfort helped me climb through the opening into the fire pit. I knelt there in pitch-darkness until he extended his lantern inside.

Over the years, rain and snow had flowed down through the chimney and packed the ashes into a hard coating beneath my feet.

"I'll need something to dig with," I said.

Leaving the lantern in the opening, Major de Monfort went off for a minute, coming back with the head of one of the spades I had seen earlier on the floor.

Grasping it tightly in both hands, I began striking at the hard coal-and-ash mixture, which was now almost like cement. As I worked, it was impossible to escape the horrible vision of Corporal Blewitt digging equally furiously at the graves around Fairfield Hall in his own quest to solve the riddle. Was I now truly at the point of learning the final answer?

TWENTY-FIVE

A FEW INCHES BELOW the surface I found the first crate. In fact, I smashed down so hard on it with the head of the shovel that the blade went right through the rotted wooden lid and I literally struck gold.

Lieutenant Shawnessy had packed the boxes side by side in the ruined fire pit and then buried them under a thick layer of ashes. The crates were almost four feet long, a foot and a half wide, and eighteen inches high. They were made of thick pine boards strapped with iron bands. It was when we tried to move them that I realized just how strong a man Donegal Shawnessy must have been. The three of us together were unable to lift even one of the crates out of the forge.

That was when Major de Monfort said he was going back for the wagon. He asked us to move the bars one by one to a place along the side of the building where we could repack them directly into the wagon upon his return. He told us not to worry if it took him several hours to get back. He was planning to muffle the horses' hooves with blanket sleeves, he said, and expected to go very slowly to avoid making undue noise.

As soon as he left, Kate and I began the arduous task of

moving the gold bars from the fire pit to the place where Major de Monfort hoped to back up the wagon. She remained outside while I carried the bars to her at the window and she stacked them on the ground. It took us almost two hours to empty the crates from the fire pit.

There were ninety-two gold bars in all, spread almost equally between the three boxes. The bars themselves were rectangular in shape with square-cut sides, about eight inches long and two inches wide. There was no imprint on them to indicate where they came from. Each one was pale yellow and much heavier than any object I had ever lifted of that size. There were also three large cloth bags labeled U. S. Army, and each one of them was filled with Federal greenbacks. We didn't take the time then to count just how much.

When we were finished, we sat down together to await his return. In spite of my excitement, I must have fallen asleep, because the next thing I remember was Kate nudging my shoulder.

"Someone is coming," she whispered excitedly.

Cocking the Sharps rifle, she rested the barrel on her left knee and aimed it down the road. We waited in the darkness as the faint steps became loud enough to be recognized as the muffled hoofbeats of Major de Monfort's wagon team. Kate put down the rifle and rushed toward him as he stepped down from the wagon.

"Alain," she said as they briefly embraced.

"We have little time to spare," he said. "It will soon be light."

Working together, we quickly loaded the wagon and were soon on our way. Unfortunately, the wagon now sagged badly from its heavy burden. It creaked and groaned with each step the horses took. In order to lighten the load, the major got down and walked. Over his quiet protest, Kate joined him on foot while I took over the reins.

Every harsh noise we made on the trip back was exaggerated

in my mind to a clamorous roar. I soon convinced myself that not only McQuade and his gang, but the whole Yankee army would be onto us before we came to the next turn in the road. Our luck held, however, and as light began to come up in the east, we rolled back into our camp next to the deep cut.

I was all for heading south right then, but the major said it would be foolhardy to travel in daylight, and Kate agreed with him. They decided we should rest again that day and leave as soon as it got dark.

For the last time, we unharnessed the horses and hobbled them in the small clearing. After we had eaten, Kate brought out the jug of spirits we had brought from the house. With great ceremony, she poured us each a small quantity of the amber liquid.

Tapping her cup against each of ours, she said solemnly, "May this war soon be over."

I said, "To my father and his men and what this gold will mean to their new lives."

The major said nothing. We all emptied our cups. I immediately volunteered to stand guard, but was secretly grateful when Major de Monfort said he wasn't tired and would take the first watch.

With weary satisfaction, Kate and I climbed into the wagon. I could not help grinning at the realization we had recovered the gold and would soon be heading south to Richmond. My last waking thought was the notion that I would actually meet General Robert E. Lee.

TWENTY-SIX

IT WAS LATE MORNING when we awoke to nothing short of a revelation. As I write these words, I feel yet again the thrill of discovering that incredible secret. Before falling asleep just a few hours earlier, I remembered seeing Major de Monfort on the far side of the clearing, standing alone like a guardian angel, just as he had been my protector so many times before.

Now, he was no longer alone. There were two men with him and I recognized one of them right away. It was Mr. Gamage. He and the major were standing together and quietly conversing on the other side of the clearing. The second man was a Negro, as destitute in aspect as I have ever seen. He was dressed in an assemblage of clothing scraps, and his footgear consisted of two furry animal pelts that were wrapped around his feet and tied in place with drapery cords.

Yet, somehow he too looked familiar, and it took only a moment to remember him as well. He was the man who was sitting on the porch at the store near Gainesville where Major de Monfort had bought the tallow for our lanterns.

When the major looked up and saw me gazing at him in wonder, he began walking toward me. Mr. Gamage came with him.

"I believe you already know my colleague," he said with a warm smile. I nodded coldly. Kate was aroused by the voices and sat up next to me.

"You both deserve to know why this gold is not going to General Lee," the major said calmly. "And why it is going north to Washington."

His statement left me speechless.

"My colleagues will be taking it through the Union lines later this morning. I will then fulfill the pledge I made to you, Katharine."

"Why?" was all I could muster.

"It is going to the Freedmen's Bureau, Jamie," he said. "The money will help resettle thousands of former slaves who are now living in squalid camps all around the Capitol, subjected to degradation you cannot imagine."

"Who are you?" said Kate.

"I have played many roles in the last four years, Katharine."

"You are not Major Alain de Monfort," she said.

"There is no Major de Monfort," he replied.

"And your life growing up in Louisiana?" she asked.

"That part of the story is true. I was born and raised in the Bayou La Frenière," he said. "But I was born a slave."

"You're a Negro?" I said in astonishment.

"My mother was from Jamaica," he said. "My father . . . well, my father was descended from an ancient French family that claims Marshal Ney as one of our forebears. My father owned Château La Frenière along with ten thousand acres of Louisiana cotton lands."

"And you were raised as a slave?" asked Kate.

"My mother was his slave, as was I. However, I was fortunate to be educated with my half brothers. I received classical training in Latin as well as lessons in swordsmanship from a former officer of the Napoleonic Guard. I was quite a good student," he said with a grin.

"And then?" she asked.

"And then I became a slave-stealer."

"Yes," she said, as if it all now made sense to her.

"The chevalier freed me on his deathbed three years before the war began. I came north. In Boston I met a man named Frederick Douglass. Not long afterward I was inspired to begin stealing slaves and helping to bring them north to freedom."

"How did you lose your arm?" I demanded, still not able to reconcile my feelings for the man he now said he was from the Confederate hero I believed him to be.

"Jamie, it was an honorable wound," he said. "I was bringing a group of men north from Mississippi and was shot by a bounty man. That part of me is buried in Benton, Missouri."

"And the house with the runaways?" asked Kate.

"A stop on the Underground Railroad, Katharine. Mr. Gamage is one of our most stalwart conductors and the bravest man I know."

Right then I had never heard of the Underground Railroad and had no idea what he was talking about. Kate obviously did because she just nodded in understanding.

"You have not met my other colleague," said the man I still called the major, as he brought over the Negro man.

"Underneath this hideous costume is my friend Father James Donaldson, late of the mathematics department at Georgetown College in Washington."

He must have seen the doubt in my eyes because his next words were, "Georgetown is a Jesuit college, Jamie. The Jesuits do not allow the pigment of a man's skin to intrude on his ability to do the Lord's work."

"And the learning of calculus often requires divine intervention," said the Negro man with a grin. He held out his hand to me and I found myself shaking it. Behind the heavy beard, his eyes were clear and intelligent.

"What will you do now?" asked Kate, who appeared completely indifferent to his new plans for the gold.

"After dark we shall head south away from Sudley Springs," he said. "Then over to Groveton and on to Manassas. The place where I shall leave my colleagues is just beyond the spur of the Orange and Alexandria Railroad. It is a safe route from there to Washington. When they are on their way, I shall return with you and Jamie to plan a trap for Captain McQuade and his men. I hope that is all right, Katharine."

"Why can't we wait here?" I asked, already thinking that as soon as he left, I would try to find some Confederate soldiers to help me get the gold back.

With a rueful smile, he said, "I regret that until the gold is safely on its way, we shall all have to stay together." It was his polite way of saying he didn't trust me.

During the rest of that last afternoon, the three of them worked to disguise what they would be carrying from any casual search on the way to Washington. While James Donaldson went off carrying a hatchet, the major and Mr. Gamage emptied the wagon and removed its canvas top and support frame. Next, they spread the gold bars out in a single layer on the wooden planks of the bed. Then, they flattened out the money sacks and placed them under the seat. Finally, they covered it all again with the canvas top.

By then, James Donaldson had returned with a huge bundle of kindling wood tied to the back of a mule. After removing it, he left to gather more. Mr. Gamage began to carefully place the kindling in layers on top of the canvas, while the major spread a blanket on the ground and began to examine the loads in each of their weapons. He did not ask for my help and I did not offer any. I was thus greatly angered when, without even talking to me, Kate sat down on the blanket next to him.

"What is your name?" she asked.

"François Guillaume Mouton La Frenière," he said with a laugh. "I was called William."

"William," she repeated softly. I had to walk away then or risk confronting the one ally I still had with a bitter reminder of her betrayal.

By the time they were finished with their preparations, the afternoon light was failing quickly. I had to admit they had done a good job of converting the wagon. It now looked like nothing more than a conveyance of firewood to the fuel-starved citizens of Washington.

It turned out Mr. Gamage had brought three mules with him and two of them were now harnessed to the wagon. After they saddled the horses, the major told us his final plans.

He, Kate, and I were to ride ahead of the wagon on horseback until we reached the spur of the Orange and Alexandria Railroad. Mr. Gamage would drive the mule team and James Donaldson would bring up the rear on the third mule.

Since we would now be moving away from Sudley Springs, the major said it was very unlikely we would run into any of McQuade's gang. Nevertheless, he urged them to be on their guard for anything. James Donaldson was looking a little uneasy and the major put his arm reassuringly around his shoulder.

"I guess you would much rather be imparting a theorem in Georgetown right now," he said.

"I will have the rest of my life to be a professor," said James Donaldson with a brave grin. "How often does one have a chance to be a philanthropist?"

TWENTY-SEVEN

THERE WAS STILL a hint of day-light in the western sky when we started off, following the edge of the deep cut to the southwest. The major walked his horse at a slow, steady pace. Mr. Gamage followed at the same speed, keeping the wagon in position about fifty feet behind us. James Donald-son remained another fifty feet or so behind him.

At the first road we came to, the major led us east on a new track. About a mile later we turned south onto a larger lane that he said would take us to the railroad spur. We never got there.

The major was the first one to notice the wagon had stopped behind us. We turned our horses in the lane and looked back. It was already too dark to see his face, but Mr. Gamage was waving at us to come to him with his right arm. I couldn't see James Donaldson at all.

The major drew his revolver from his belt and then let it hang at his side, hidden behind his leg. With the reins in his teeth, he started walking his horse back down the road. We followed a few feet behind.

As we drew close enough to see him more clearly, it appeared to me that Mr. Gamage was silently laughing at us. I did not know then it was because his throat had been cut from ear to ear. Nor did I realize that the arm which was waving at us was not his.

Everything that happened next took place faster than I am able to write it down. With a sudden motion, the major raised his pistol and fired at Mr. Gamage. At almost the same moment, two more explosions rang out. From the corner of my eye, I saw the muzzle flashes off to the right. Then the major hurtled backward out of the saddle.

The man who was propping up Mr. Gamage on the seat of the wagon shoved his body to the side and stood up. It was Claude Moomaw, his buckskin tunic now drenched red.

Although he had lost his Colt revolver in the fall, the major was on his feet an instant later and running toward the wagon. Off to the right, two figures emerged from the darkness of the tree line, firing as they came. The major staggered as he was hit again, going down for the second time. He rolled in the dirt and somehow came up on his feet. Considering he had at least two bullets in him, I don't know how he moved so fast.

Kate was now off her horse and scrabbling on her hands and knees in the dirt. From way down the road, another wraith-like figure loomed out of the darkness and closed on the wagon. It became James Donaldson. He was shouting something to the major in the moment before he fell, shot from behind. Thurman came up after him, his rifle pointed forward as the major reached the team of mules.

Oblivious to this new threat, he was reaching behind his neck just as Thurman leveled his rifle at him from a distance of less than five feet. Then, another shot rang out and Thurman dropped the rifle, falling to his knees. I turned to see Kate, who was now standing straight as a ramrod. She had retrieved the major's revolver and it was extended from her outstretched hand.

Now, the major was vaulting into the wagon, the Louisiana toothpick in his hand. Claude was still standing up behind the seat, bellowing at the top of his lungs, as he raised his pistol and fired. The major thrust his sword deep into Claude's groin, slicing upward as the old tracker fired again from point-blank range.

The men who had come out of the tree line from off to the right swung around at the sound of Kate's shot. One of them was Dex, and in a smooth practiced way he brought his rifle to his shoulder and took aim at her.

I kicked my horse in the flanks to move between them, but before the animal could react, I heard another explosion and the rifle sailed out of Dex's outflung arms. A moment later his body lurched after it, stumbling twice, before he fell hard on his face in the dirt.

Behind him stood Captain McQuade, his gun still pointing at where Dex had been standing. As I watched, his gun hand dropped to his side.

"Enough," he said in the sudden quiet. "That's enough."

The whole thing had taken less than thirty seconds, and it ended the lives of five men, not including Mr. Gamage, who was already dead.

Claude and the major were still alive when I got to the wagon. The old Indian fighter was down on his knees behind the seat, making harsh guttural noises like a rooting boar as he tried to hold his intestines in.

The major was lying on his back in the road. By the time I reached his side, Kate already had his head cradled under her right arm and was gently stroking the hair away from his eyes.

"When it is all over," he said, the words trickling out in the familiar lilting accent, "please write to Frederick Douglass . . . just tell him . . . I am gone."

His eyes focused on Katharine's. He raised his hand from the dirt and I watched it hover for a moment at her cheek before falling away.

"Adieu," he said. His eyes were still on hers when all the life ebbed out of them.

As Kate passed her hand over his face, I found myself crying. It's hard now to remember the reasons why. After all, he had lied to me and then tried to steal the gold. But none of that mattered just then. I somehow knew I had lost something far more important than the gold.

We were still kneeling next to him in the mud when Claude called out in a hoarse voice, "What was his name?"

The tracker had fallen over to the side of the wagon. Just his shaggy head and bulbous nose could be seen over the seat, his expression wildly distorted.

"Tell me who he was," he demanded again, but by the time Kate replied, I think he was already dead.

"William," she said.

TWENTY-EIGHT

WE LEFT THEM ALL lying where they were. In the wake of the gunfire, it was certain that the Yankees would soon be along to investigate. I brought matters to a head.

It may sound stupid, but I went over to the major's horse and removed the Sharps rifle from his saddle holster. Then, I turned to face Captain McQuade and pointed it at his heart.

"I'm taking this gold through the Confederate lines to General Lee," I said. "You can take your horse and go if you want. I won't try to stop you. But if you try to interfere with me in any way, I will shoot you down."

Maybe it was because he was finally sickened by all the violence he had wrought, but Captain McQuade seemed completely listless. He had already dropped his gun to the ground and just stood there by the road, wearily shaking his head.

"That may be the best idea after all, Jamie," he said.

I picked up his pistol and shoved it in my belt. Kate continued to kneel by the major while I dragged Claude Moomaw out of the wagon and dropped his corpse to the ground. Blood was everywhere, and I mopped it up as best I could before spreading two blankets across the seat.

There was no resistance when I gently grasped Kate by the shoulders and helped her to climb back in the buckboard. Captain McQuade had already mounted one of the horses. He walked him up beside us as I grabbed the harness reins in my hands.

"If you don't mind, I think I'll ride along for a while," he said.

He had not attempted to pick up any of the weapons scattered on the ground, and I just shrugged at him before snapping the reins. We headed off into the night.

Kate never spoke through the long journey that followed. To my knowledge she never slept. She sat almost rigidly straight, staring forward, lost in her thoughts. Her face was like a stone mask.

The only time I exchanged words with Captain McQuade was when I asked him how they had found us and he told me that Thurman had been watching one of the lanes we had taken back to our camp after retrieving the gold. He had followed us there, and then gone back to the others, after which they had planned their ambush.

It was pitch-dark when we got to Groveton. I turned the mules south. In the next fourteen hours, we crossed the Manassas Gap Railroad line and forded Broad Run near Bristoe, before riding on through Catlett's Station. Then I used the major's compass to follow a string of country roads that brought us through nameless sleeping settlements, drawing ever closer to the city of Fredericksburg. My plan was to find a place on its outskirts to lay up long enough to rest the mules before a final push down to the Confederate lines at Richmond.

It began to rain about midnight and came down hard

through the rest of that night. We were stopped twice on the journey, once by Yankee sentries at Catlett's Station and later by a small unit guarding Kelly's Ford along the Rappahannock River near Richardsville.

On each occasion, I explained that we were carrying firewood to sell in Fredericksburg. Maybe it was the listless, bedraggled appearance of Captain McQuade and me or, perhaps, it was the sadness in Kate's eyes, but each time they held up the lanterns to our faces, the sentries allowed us to pass.

At Kelly's Ford, a corporal in command of the sentries did order his men to search the wagon, but they just poked their bayonets into the kindling pile to make sure there was no one hiding inside.

It was almost seven the next morning when we arrived at a place where it was clear another titanic battle had once been fought. As at Manassas, the first sign could be found in the torn and sundered trees. Then we began to see the discarded wreckage of battle. Large animal bones and mangled military equipment littered both sides of the road for miles.

I asked Captain McQuade if he knew the name of the battle that had been fought there.

"Chancellorsville," he said.

"Were you there?" I asked and he nodded without speaking.

We came to a large intersecting crossroad heading west to east. On my right I saw the brick remains of a massive building that had burned to its foundations. The ground cover around it was completely torn away as if the soldiers fighting there had not been satisfied until every living thing was ripped from the earth. I asked the captain if the new road led into Fredericksburg and he said yes. I urged the exhausted mules forward and headed east.

We were only a few miles from the outskirts of the city when a growing clatter behind us revealed itself to be a mounted Yankee patrol. They were still a hundred yards back, but coming on at full gallop. I was about to pull over to the side of the road when one of the lead riders fired his pistol into the air.

"Give those mules the whip, Jamie," shouted Captain McQuade. "They mean to search you for sure."

Without hesitation, I snapped the reins onto the rumps of the poor mules and they began to speed up. A moment later, I realized there was no way to outrun our pursuers, and cursed myself for having listened to him.

"Throw me the Sharps," he yelled, as he cantered his horse in close beside us, no more than three feet away. Kate still seemed oblivious to everything that was happening, and it was now too late for me to pursue another course. If they caught up to us now, they were sure to discover what we were carrying. I reached down with my right hand and tossed the rifle into his outstretched hand.

In one fluid motion, he swung around in the saddle, aimed and fired. Although one of the cavalrymen fell away from his mount, it had no impact on the others. There were a score of them at least, and they never slowed for an instant. Now, as they returned his fire, I heard one ball tear through the kindling stacked behind us.

My first thought then was of Kate's safety and I was about to stop the mules when from up ahead of us there was a thin crackle of musket fire, followed by four curls of smoke. The flashes came from a distant line of old fortifications that ran from north to south ahead of us. I looked back to see another one of the pursuing riders drop from his horse. This time the rest pulled up short.

I turned off the road into the field on our left and headed the mules in the direction of the friendly fire. The wagon began to shake so hard over the uneven ground that I wondered if we would make it to the trench line without disaster. Less than a minute later, however, we crested the low sloping hill at the

edge of the trench and careened to a stop in the woods just beyond. Captain McQuade thundered in behind us a few seconds
later.

My first thought when I looked back along the vast fortifications was that they were utterly empty. Obviously long abandoned, they now appeared to be no more than a sea of mud. But
I knew someone had to be there and finally we saw them. Four
lonely figures lying along the highest trench line.

"Heah," one of them called out. "Ovuh heah."

I helped Kate out of the wagon. As we struggled through the
mud, Captain McQuade tried to take her arm but she brushed
his hand away as if it were diseased. We finally reached their position along the trench line and crouched down under the log
parapet they were lying behind.

The man closest to me looked like Robinson Crusoe come
to life, with long stringy hair and a scraggly beard. He stuck out
a dirt-encrusted hand and said, "Sergeant Buck Wampler . . .
Them goddam Yanks down ta killing us for firewood?"

"We've got something they would want if they knew we had
it," I said, giving his hand a shake although it hurt to do so. He
must not have been a curious man for he asked me nothing
further about it.

I had often read the letters from my father in which he re-
ferred to his men as scarecrows. These soldiers were that living
image, although there was a lean, sinewy toughness to them as
well.

The face of the man crouching next to Sergeant Wampler
was the color of a new pumpkin and it took me a moment to
realize he was yellow with jaundice. That may have accounted
for his ornery humor.

"Back in a goddam trench," he exclaimed. "The whole goddam reason we left Petersburg and look at us now. Right back
where we started from."

"You've come from Petersburg?" I said, and he nodded.

The third soldier in the line looked away, maybe ashamed of having left his comrades. He was younger than the others and had good teeth.

"I done my share of killin'," he said to no one in particular. "Three years' worth."

"Were you anywhere near the 10th Virginia?" I asked anxiously.

"I don't rightly know," said Sergeant Wampler. "But you kin bet they's there. The whole goddam army's there. You got kin with the 10th?"

I said yes.

"He'll be all right. Only danger rat now is from a cave-in."

"No more diggin' fer me," declared the last man, who wore rimless spectacles.

"They made us into mole men," said Sergeant Wampler. "Hell's fire, we wasn't sojers no more. All they had us do was dig . . . forts, goddam saylents, covered trenches, zigzag trenches, you name it. They had us livin' like worms down there."

"It give me the plague," said the yellow-skinned man.

"The ague, Jesse," said Sergeant Wampler. "The ague."

"Same difference, Buck," he replied.

"Them bluebellies was dug in so close if'n ah had a biscuit I reckon I coulda thrown it right over the Yank line," said the young one.

"Ah reckon ah'm a sojer, not a badger," said the soldier in spectacles.

"Where are you from?" I asked Sergeant Wampler.

He grinned, uncovering a mouthful of broken brown-stained teeth.

"I come all the way from First Manassas," he said. "July the twenty-first, 1861."

A bullet whizzed loudly through the air and struck the earthen bank behind me with a loud thunk. It was still hot to the touch when I dug it out and rubbed the dirt off on my shirt cuff. It was almost an inch long and conical in shape, with two ridged lines around the base.

"They still usin' those old muzzle-loadin' Enfields," said the jaundiced soldier. "Fifty-eight-caliber rifled slug. Take yer leg right off."

As we watched, a few of the Yankees started into the field in front of us. Then the men stopped as if their orders had been changed and they went back to the road.

"Where are you headed?" asked Captain McQuade.

"Over to Romney. We's all from around there," said the sergeant. "Camped back in those woods last night."

"Who you think we got over there?" asked the spectacled soldier.

"Regular cav'ry, looks like."

"One way to find out," said Sergeant Wampler. Cupping his filthy hands together, he yelled out, "Who is you people?"

"Thirty-third New Yawk Cavalry," came back a nasal brass-lunged voice.

"Nooo Yokuhs. They's the wust," said Sergeant Wampler, shaking his woolly head. "No manners, them people. Always crowin' bout this or that."

"Come on out here, Johnny," yelled back the same voice. "We'll meet ya halfway."

Off to our left, I could see the spire of an old weather-beaten church, its shingled belfry holed in several places by cannon shot. Turning to look behind us, I saw what appeared to be a narrow lane snaking back through the woods.

"You got any tobacco, Johnny?" came the nasal voice again.

"Two sacks," was the shouted reply.

"Well, you keep it dry for us," the voice yelled back.

"You'all jes come on n' git it."

Most of the Yankees were now just milling around way down the road, as if still waiting to be told what to do.

"Them boys is green as a Yankee dollar," said the spectacled soldier. He wasn't even looking at them anymore, having sat down with his back against the log. He had pulled out a piece of wood and was whittling at it with a small narrow-bladed buck knife.

"You look like you was an officer," said Sergeant Wampler to Captain McQuade.

"Was is correct," he replied.

"What outfit?"

"33rd Virginia," he said.

"Nothuh of Stonewall's boys," said the yellow man. "Evuh meet him?"

McQuade nodded. "Yes, I did," he said.

"I seen him onct too. It was afore I jined the army. He come to Romney in the middle of a blizzard in January of sixty-two. Them boys of his was sore at him right then I can tell you . . . He was sittin' on a little spindly horse, he was. Biggest feet I ever saw in boot leather."

"Ah don't car one hoot about his feet," said the sergeant. "Ah jes wisht we'd a had him at Gettysburg insteada ol' Peg Leg Ewell. Jackson woulda tak'n that hah ground the fust day we was there n' the war woulda bin ovah rat then. That's when we lost the whole shebang."

"You may be right about that," said Captain McQuade with a grim smile.

The Yankees were still standing around in the road, although as I watched, three more rode up behind a trooper carrying a red and gold guidon.

"I got to say this," said the whittler. "They survived all them lousy gin'rals. Pope n' Banks n' Burnside . . . Spent those boys like donkeys n' they still come back for more."

I could now hear an officer's voice in full pitch, shouting orders at the men milling about in the road. More than a dozen of them moved into the field in a skirmish line and began to slowly trudge in our direction. At the same time, I saw another group of soldiers begin moving into the trees on the other side of the road.

"They gonna try to outflank us," said Sergeant Wampler.

"Won't be hard," said the yellow man.

As the skirmish line moved forward, the soldiers flushed a covey of grackles from the tall grass, and they took off to the west. That was when I heard the sound of a hornpipe. It came from one of the soldiers who was still waiting with the horses back down the road. He was playing a fast, spirited version of "When Johnny Comes Marching Home."

"Brung their own goddam band with 'em," said Sergeant Wampler, spitting out tobacco juice.

"Probably their first time in a scrap," said the whittler. "They all want somethin' to write home about."

"I'll give 'em somethin'," said the youngest one, resting his musket on the log in front of him and taking aim.

"Won't be long now," said Sergeant Wampler, looking toward the flankers moving behind the other line of fortifications across the road. "You better git out of it if yer goin.' They's a dozen trails through those woods back there where you kin lose 'em sure. After that, it's clear all the way to Richmond. Grant's gittin' all his supplies up the James. Ain't no one northa Richmond 'sept peckerheads like these."

"Why don't you get out with us?" I said, taking Kate's hand and helping her to her feet.

"We ain't never run from a fight," he replied, standing up behind the log breastwork. "And I ain't gonna make this one from behind no goddam trench," he held forth. One of the Yankee skirmishers fired at him and the bullet slammed into the redoubt behind us with a loud slap.

"I would be proud to lead you, Sergeant," said Captain McQuade. For the first time, Kate looked up from the ground as he walked slowly toward his horse.

"Well, boys, we got us an officer again who leads from up front," said the yellow soldier.

The spectacled man stood up and grabbed his musket.

"Here," he said, tossing the piece of wood he had been whittling over to me.

The figure was of a perfectly sculpted screech owl. I was amazed at the intricate, lifelike detail of its upper plumage and the distinctive ears. As I pen these words, it is lying on the table in front of me.

I ran to catch up to Captain McQuade. As he swung up into the saddle, I heard a low unguarded sigh escape his lips. Bespattered with mud, he raised his eyes toward the line of Yankee skirmishers and then glanced down at me. The glints of gold in his black irises stood out and they reminded me again of lion's eyes. I held his pistol up to him but he shook his head, saying, "You keep it, Jamie. Might come in handy."

I didn't know what to say to him then, and he seemed to understand that. "I'm sorry about the way it all turned out," he said, touching his fingers to his wide-brimmed hat.

Spurring his horse forward, he rode back down the hill toward the others. I was helping Kate climb back into the wagon when I heard the sergeant's voice.

"Mah name's Buck Wampler," he was bellowing almost loud enough to be heard in Richmond, "n' I kin lick any man in Morgan County."

There was shouting from the Yankees too, as Captain Mc-Quade led the others past the trench line and headed toward them. Somehow, the four Confederates no longer looked like tramps as they crossed the field, bent low to the ground as several of the skirmishers opened fire.

McQuade looked back just once. I waved to him but I don't believe he saw me before turning to face the Federal fire. That was when the other four gave out with the Rebel yell. It was the last time I ever heard it.

The first time I heard one was during the Battle of Port Republic when the Louisiana boys roared it each time they charged up the ravine below our house to try to take the Yankee cannons. Back then they had sounded like a thousand hogs in a slaughter pen all screaming as one. This Rebel yell was just a faint echo but horrific just the same.

The skirmishers halted in their tracks and discharged a ragged volley with no apparent effect. As they worked to reload, Captain McQuade expertly lifted his horse over a gully and began galloping straight toward them. He was carrying the Sharps rifle straight up on his knee.

Behind him, the four Confederates were now running flat out with their bayonets pointed forward, still screaming at the top of their lungs. When they were no more than ten yards away, the fifteen Yankees actually turned and began to run. A few of them dropped their weapons as they flew.

Kate never looked back as I slapped the reins and the mules began to move toward the tree line. For those next few seconds there was no more firing, and thinking back on it, I believe it was because the soldiers farther down the road were afraid of hitting their own men.

When I turned again, the skirmishers were almost back to where they had started from. McQuade was way out in front of the others when the next volley came from the Yankee line. A cloud of gunsmoke drifted toward us across the field and I saw the spectacled man go down. Sergeant Wampler and the other two were still on their feet, leaning forward now as if facing into a buffeting wind while they reloaded their muskets.

Kate and I were at the tree line when I looked back for the last time. Two of the three remaining Confederates had used the brief lull after their successful charge to slip off toward the bunker line to the right. Sergeant Wampler still stood his ground in the middle of the field as bullets tore up the earth around him. He was yelling at the captain, who continued heading toward the Federal line.

"You goddam fool," came back on the wind. A second later he was running after his friends.

McQuade was all by himself now, his horse walking slowly but steadily toward the Yankees, the Sharps rifle balanced on his knee. Maybe some of them thought he was too brave to shoot. I don't know. But then I heard more yelling. Right after that there was another ragged volley.

I never saw the result. At the same moment, I felt a stunning blow in my right arm. It whirled me around into Kate and almost propelled me out of the wagon. I knew right away I was shot and that it must have come from one of the flankers who had come up along the other side of the road.

Kate kept me from falling under the wagon. Grabbing the reins, she cried, "Oh God, Jamie, say you're all right."

I remembered the heft of that fifty-eight-caliber minié ball and was almost frightened to look at my arm. Glancing down, I saw that the bullet had torn away a large piece of my coat and gone straight through my upraised shoulder. It was already bleeding a lot but as yet there was no pain at all.

"I'm all right," I said, and her eyes relaxed again. By then, we were already into the sanctuary of the piney woods and moving at a good clip. Sergeant Wampler had been telling the truth. The forest was a regular rabbit warren of logging roads and trails leading in every possible direction. Kate kept going for more than a mile, taking different paths until she felt sure we could not be followed.

Finally, she stopped the wagon and tended to my shoulder. It was still bleeding freely as she tightly bound the wound with a strip of lining torn from the inside of her coat.

That night we slept in a grove of walnut trees near Spotsylvania Court House. The next morning we pushed on again toward Richmond.

TWENTY-NINE

WELL, THAT'S PRETTY much the whole story, except for what happened to the gold. On the afternoon of the third day of our journey, we arrived at the outer line of Confederate fortifications north of Richmond.

It had started snowing again that morning, and by the time we got there the landscape was completely white once more. I was feeling very poorly by then. The wound in my shoulder ached terribly and I began to suspect it was worse than I had first thought.

It turned out there were no regular troops manning the fortifications. In fact, there was nobody there at all. I remembered Sergeant Wampler telling us that General Grant was putting all his effort to break through the Confederate lines way down near Petersburg. Still, it seemed strange they didn't have anyone north of Richmond.

The mystery was cleared up when we reached the second line of trenches and came upon scores of men gathered around the half-butchered carcass of an emaciated horse. Two of them were frantically hacking away chunks of flesh and bone and then passing them back to the rest.

There was no effort made to dress the meat. Less than twenty feet away from the dead animal, they had started a fire and the lucky ones who had already received their ration were roasting it on the points of their bayonets.

Kate stopped to ask directions a little farther on and was told that the fortifications in this sector were being manned by one of the Richmond Home Guard units. From what I saw, it consisted mostly of old men and cripples.

We had just cleared the last interior line of fortifications when there was a loud cracking noise and the right rear wheel broke free from the wagon. As we ground to an immediate halt, the bed of the buckboard tipped so far over to the side that I was worried the gold bars would spill out onto the roadway. I climbed down to look at the extent of the damage, and saw that the rear axle was smashed beyond repair.

I despaired at the thought of how we could possibly locate another wagon and then transfer the gold to it without being observed. The road we were on was the principal route for supplies to this part of the front, and even though there was no enemy activity, the chances of concealing what we needed to do were almost impossible.

Taking the risk of leaving the buckboard unattended in the road, I asked a boy who was passing by if he knew where we might find the commander of the Home Guard. He led us to what looked from the outside like a beaver's den. It was built directly into the side of a high earthen mound that formed part of the interior defense line.

At the base of the mound there was a rope-hinged door fashioned from undressed pine boards. Our young escort gently rapped on it. After waiting thirty seconds without any response, he tried again.

"What is it now?" came an angry voice from within. Wincing, the boy summoned his nerve to speak.

"Two people asking to see you, Colonel Twombly. Their wagon just broke down coming through the lines."

"Do I have to do everything around here?" came back the voice. "Let Lieutenant Cooksey handle it!"

The boy was turning to leave when I brushed past him and threw open the door. Inside the hovel, the air was warm from a log fire, but foul with the smell of sweat and putrefaction. A candle guttered on a plank board that was suspended between two flour barrels. In the far corner, a man was lying on a camp cot under several blankets. He struggled to his feet as Kate followed me inside and shut the door.

"What is the meaning of this?" he demanded. Although bald as an egg, his face had strong manly features.

"We are carrying a vitally important shipment for General Lee," I said.

He looked us up and down and then frowned. Admittedly, our appearance could not have inspired confidence in that assertion.

"A few bales of hay, I suppose . . . and available to the army for a fair price," he said with sarcasm in his voice.

If my arm wasn't on fire with pain, I know I would not have said what I did next.

"There are ninety-two gold bars outside in the wagon, and I am delivering them to my father, who is commanding the 10th Virginia under General Lee."

From his smug grin I knew right away he didn't believe me. It was only when Kate removed the shawl covering her head and stepped forward into the feeble candlelight that his manner suddenly changed.

"He's telling you the truth," she said with the old Dandridge spirit I had come to know so well.

I gave him only the barest elements of the story. When I was finished, we walked outside so he could look for himself at what was under the snow-covered canvas. He immediately ordered several men to guard the buckboard while we went back inside.

"I am Colonel Hubert Twombly," he declared with a suddenly expansive smile. "Formerly of the provost marshal's staff and currently enjoying the signal honor of commanding this section of the front against the Yankee invaders."

He stuck his hand out to show there were no hard feelings. When I did not respond, he glanced at my arm and said, "Why, you're hurt. That should be tended to right away. I will have you escorted to—"

"That can wait," I said, cutting him short. "Right now, Colonel, I would like your assistance in transferring the gold to another wagon so we can carry it on to my father and General Lee."

"Of course, of course," he said. "Well, you have definitely found the right man," he said. Going to his plank table, he sat down on a cracker box and began scribbling on a piece of paper. When he was finished and went to fold it, I saw it was written on the back of a piece of sheet music. He carefully sealed the edges with hot tallow. Then, he stood up.

"You both wait right here by the fire," he said in a solicitous manner.

Going to the door, he swung it open and called out, "Lieutenant Cooksey!"

A boy no older than me appeared at the door.

"Take our fastest horse and deliver this to Colonel Wilson," he said. "You are to wake him if necessary and personally place this letter in his hands. No one else is to read it, is that clear?"

"Yes, sir," he said, rushing off.

Colonel Twombly came back inside, shutting the door behind him.

"Please sit down," he said cheerfully. When he did not renew his offer to send for a doctor, Kate reminded him of my wound and he went outside again to send for one.

"It may take some time," he said when he returned. "We are rather stretched thin here at the front, as you can well imagine."

While we waited, Colonel Twombly kept up a lively conversation. Mostly, it was about himself and his service to the Confederacy. Before the war, he said, he was just a simple country lawyer in Culpeper who enjoyed nothing more than providing honest legal representation to the good people of the Piedmont. After that he had been blessed with the privilege of serving a term in the state legislature before an unfortunate incident led to his defeat at the next election. He told us what it was but I can't remember now. When the war came, he volunteered his services immediately, and was assigned to the provost marshal's office, where he was responsible for providing rations to the captured Federal troops confined in Confederate prison camps. He said he had received numerous commendations from General Winder himself.

At one point, I interrupted him to ask who Colonel Wilson was.

"He is the perfect man for this job," he said. "Very discreet, shall we say."

I told him again that the gold was bound for General Lee to help the army, and he said not to worry. It would get there in due course.

An hour later, two men in long black frock coats knocked on the door and said they had come for the shipment. The first one looked like our undertaker in Port Republic. He did all the talking.

I asked who they were and he said they were from the commissary general's office, serving under General Mayberry. He then told me I would be given a receipt for the gold and later on I would receive a letter of commendation from General Mayberry himself.

I said I had never heard of General Mayberry, and wanted the gold taken directly to General Lee. He responded that I was ignorant of army regulations and should desist from trying to hector the men chosen to carry out this important responsibility.

When I persisted, the first one became visibly angry and said he would ride to the office of Jefferson Davis, and return with an order from the president himself. I must confess that this took me down a few pegs and I reluctantly agreed.

For the third or fourth time since we had arrived, Kate demanded to know where the doctor was. Colonel Twombly shrugged his shoulders and counseled her to be patient, saying he was doing the best he could under the circumstances.

"This is war," he said.

I could see that Kate was fed up with the whole business. She was also worried at the condition of my arm, which had swollen alarmingly during the previous few hours. She again urged me to go with her to the home of her aunt, who lived on Franklin Street, and would know exactly where to get immediate medical attention for me. Colonel Twombly strongly endorsed her suggestion and offered to have us taken there immediately. I refused.

It was well after dark and still snowing hard when the men in the black frock coats came back. They had another man with them now. This one was wearing a brand-new gray uniform with shiny gold braid down each arm. He had a small potbelly and long muttonchop whiskers. Stepping into the light, he clicked his heels together with a loud crack and said, "Captain Kunzel I am. Now I gif dis you oduh!"

He handed a sealed document to Colonel Twombly, who tore it open and read it. Then he handed the document to me. It was written in pen on the stationery of General Vernon Loveless, chief of the Quartermaster Corps, Confederate States of America.

"You are hereby ordered," it began, "to place the heretofore described shipment in the conveyance provided by this Department and have it delivered with due dispatch and adequate military escort to these offices. You are also ordered to summarily arrest any and all persons who seek to prevent you from carrying out these orders."

I looked back at Colonel Twombly, who promptly shrugged his shoulders, as if now helpless to disobey his superiors.

Enraged, I said, "The gold is going to General Lee, and if anyone tries to stop me you can answer to him."

I was turning to leave when Kate said, "Let them have it, Jamie. They will take it anyway."

Before I could respond, Lieutenant Cooksey came around the table to restrain me and roughly grabbed my wounded arm. The pain was so terrible I fell to my knees, almost fainting on the spot. A moment later, Kate had me in her arms and was asking Colonel Twombly for use of a carriage, which he readily obliged.

On the way to her aunt's house, I began vomiting. As hard as I tried to stop, my stomach and brain would not cooperate and the spasms continued all the way to her house. When they were carrying me up the front steps, I do remember thinking her aunt must be rich because the house was a mansion, and it was surrounded by others just like it.

By then, I was completely without strength. It was as if my body lacked even the force to hold the flesh to my bones. I lost consciousness before we were inside the door.

The next thing I remember was waking up in a bed with a carved headboard on it that almost touched the ceiling. I was lying between soft flannel sheets and pale moonlight was coming through the window. I could see the outline of heavy furniture against the white plaster walls and there was a cheery blaze burning in the fireplace. Then I realized someone was sitting in a chair near my bed, covered by a quilt. It took me a moment to recognize Kate, her chin dipped in slumber. I lost consciousness again.

Sometimes, it seemed very hot in the room and at other times as cold as the grave. The cold was the worst. No amount of covers could keep me from shaking like I would come apart.

One night, I thought I heard thunder and wondered whether we were having another winter storm. But, this time it was a constant rumble. Occasionally, the pounding grew so acute that the house shook and the glass teardrop crystals on the chandelier in my room actually tinkled like a wind chime. That was when I knew it wasn't thunder, but a massive artillery bombardment.

The next morning, I was awakened for my breakfast by a pretty young woman who brought me a bowl of hot beef broth. As she fed me, I was struck by her sweet smile and sorrowful eyes. Kate told me later her name was Agnes Lee and that she lived next door.

Once, I came around to hear people talking in the hallway. A man's voice was saying, "Fever has broken out. As God is my witness, Katharine, they have allowed Richmond to become a pest hole. His best chance . . ." Then I was floating away again.

It was dark outside when I awoke to find Kate sitting beside me on the edge of my bed. She was wearing a cream-colored muslin dress and her hair was pinned high around her head. The spiraling auburn curls framed her face in a perfect oval.

She was bathing my face with a cool moist towel and it felt wonderful. Yet, in the light of the oil lamp, her luminous green eyes looked stricken.

"Do not worry," I said. "It is all over now."

"Jamie, I want you to know something in case we must part for a time," she replied.

I looked up at her beautiful alabaster face and nodded.

"You are the most courageous young man I have ever known," Kate said. Then, she leaned down and kissed me full on the lips. I remember she smelled just like lilies of the valley.

At least I think she did. In the weeks since, I have relived that moment over and over. Recently, it struck me that I was in such a fevered state at the time, it all may have been just a wondrous dream.

The next time I woke up, Dr. Cassidy was by my bed. He had come to bring me home. I learned later he had ridden all the way from Port Republic to Gordonsville through Brown's Gap. There, he was lucky enough to catch one of the few remaining trains on the Virginia Central line through Louisa Court House into Richmond.

While examining my wound, he discovered that a large fragment of my coat had been driven into my arm by the Yankee bullet, where it had lodged under the clavicle and become infected. After dosing me with laudanum, he successfully removed the foreign matter, allowing the wound to drain for a time before bandaging it. By then, however, my temperature was 103 degrees and the fever had rendered me unconscious again.

According to Dr. Cassidy, the trip back to Port Republic was by far the worst he has ever experienced. If so, I'm grateful to remember almost nothing about it. I was strapped on a litter and taken in a carriage to the railroad station, where we waited all day for a train to Gordonsville. There was no longer any regularly scheduled service, and we were lucky that one eventually came. According to Dr. Cassidy, it was grossly overcrowded with people fleeing from the city and we were fortunate to find space for my litter in the baggage car. Once the train left Richmond, progress was very slow. It took three hours just to reach Hanover Junction, and another six before we got to Trevilian's Station.

Over Christmas, there had been a big fight at Gordonsville for control of the Virginia Central line. Thankfully, the Confederates still held it, but by the time we got there, Dr. Cassidy found that my temperature was 105 degrees. He told me afterward that he wasn't sure just then whether I would make it home.

From there it was an all-night journey to Charlottesville. I was in and out of consciousness during that part of the trip, and remember being told by the doctor that Sheridan's cavalry had torn up the tracks along one whole section of the line. As incredible as it sounds, the train was actually dragged by ox teams across the broken part so we could proceed. During that difficult passage, I held tight to the little gold cross Kate had given me at Christmas. The final stage of the journey took us through Rockfish Gap to Waynesboro, where a wagon was waiting to bring us the last twenty miles home.

This next part may also sound unbelievable but Dr. Cassidy swears it's true. When we arrived home and my mother rushed out of the house to greet me, she took one look at my unconscious form and said, "But where is Jamie? Where is my son?"

THIRTY

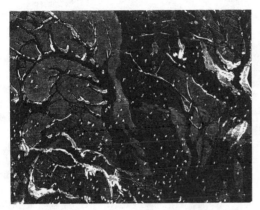

I awoke in my own bed at Port Republic two days later. Although I was still running a fever, the high temperature had broken, and Dr. Cassidy assured my mother the crisis had passed. Now, it was only a matter of getting my strength back through rest and good food, he said.

As he was leaving, he looked down at me and, with a mock frown, said, "After surviving all you've come through, Jamie, it's clear you were born to be hanged."

I didn't see the humor of the remark at the time and it must have been plain on my face. He then gave me a kindly smile. "What I meant to say," he went on, "was what Conan said to the Devil . . . 'Twas claw for claw there for a while."

I fully returned his smile, knowing I owed him my life. That was when my mother brought me a hand mirror. It was the first time I had looked into a mirror of any kind since the morning I left for Ike Trumbo's tavern.

I did not recognize myself. The face that looked back at me had sad and weary eyes, with age lines etched in both corners.

They stared at me with an intensity that was wholly unfamiliar. Even the structure of my face seemed to have changed. All the softness was gone. It took me a moment to realize I looked like a man.

I have been home now for almost a month. The first part of it was spent almost entirely in bed. Lying there all day long forced me to think hard about everything that happened to me. Until the day Corporal Blewitt came, I guess I lived mostly in my imagination, experiencing the world beyond Port Republic through books. I wonder if I can ever go back to that life now.

During these last weeks, I have had to compile this account for Judge Burwell. It's because my mother got so worried about me after I disappeared that she told Dr. Cassidy about my having gone to see Ike Trumbo with the map. He brought in Constable Kilduff, who came out with his tracking dogs and found the corporal's grave. If Dr. Cassidy hadn't stood up for her right then, they would have sworn out murder charges against both of us and branded me a fugitive. Anyway, when I'm finished writing the account, Constable Kilduff will take it over to Judge Burwell at the courthouse in Harrisonburg. If he has any doubts about whether it all really happened, I will ask him to contact Kate, who can at least confirm everything that occurred after we arrived at her father's home.

Since regaining my strength I've written a letter each day to her, but have yet to receive a response. Dr. Cassidy told me not to worry about it because everything has broken down now, including the mails. He said that to his knowledge no one west of the Blue Ridge has gotten a letter from Richmond in weeks. I can only pray she is safe and that I will see her once more.

As far as what finally happened to the gold, I don't really know anything about that either. Yesterday, Monk Shiflett was saying down at the store that Jefferson Davis has been tarred and feathered and run out of Richmond on a rail. He claims the president is now on his way to Mexico dressed as a woman. Of course, Monk passes around so much foolish talk it's a wonder anyone listens to a thing he says.

As I write these words, another winter gale is upon us. Through the gloom outside my window, I can barely see the room where Corporal Blewitt lived with us over the fruit cellar.

To my knowledge, at least fourteen men, including those Federal quartermasters, died trying to possess the gold. They all had their reasons why they were willing to give up their lives for it. I guess the major had the highest purpose in mind, although I never got the chance to ask Cole McQuade what his plans were.

If I'm not sent to prison for everything I've done, I will keep the promise we made to the major just before he died. When the war is over, I hope to travel to Washington with Kate to meet Mr. Frederick Douglass and tell him what the major tried to do.

At this point I have to assume the gold ended up in the quartermaster general's office in Richmond. The thought has occurred to me more than once that since it was Union quartermasters who took the gold in the first place, maybe it is somehow fitting that their brethren in the Confederate Army got it back in the end.

Right now, my mother is trying to keep busy in the kitchen, as she does every day, waiting for news of my father. In this, she is not alone. Perhaps tomorrow we will hear word that he is safe and coming home.

Editor's Postscript

ACCORDING TO THE National Archives in Washington, D.C., Lieutenant Colonel Thomas Lyon Lockhart, the father of James Christopher "Jamie" Lockhart, was killed helping to stem the Confederate retreat after the disaster at Sayler's Creek on April 6, 1865. In that engagement, more than eight thousand Confederate soldiers were captured, representing a loss of approximately one third of the effective strength of the Army of Northern Virginia at the time. Three days later, on Sunday, April 9, 1865, General Lee surrendered his remaining forces.

Colonel Lockhart's body was never recovered, although according to a historian at the National Park Service, his presentation sword turned up in a Cleveland pawn shop in 1926. It is now on display at the Park Service Museum in Petersburg, Virginia.

Research into the postwar lives of other individuals associated with this story was greatly impeded by the turmoil and upheaval that accompanied the Reconstruction period after President Abraham Lincoln's assassination in April 1865.

Readers might be interested to know that Jane Spenser Lockhart, the colonel's widow, eventually remarried. According to an issue of the *Rockingham County Register* dated June 14, 1867, Mrs. Lockhart became the wife of Dr. Patrick Francis Cassidy of Port Republic, presumably the same person who appears in the preceding narrative.

After looking through hundreds of letters from that period compiled by the Port Republic Historical Society, a student researcher was able to find more than a dozen references to the good works accomplished by both of them. It is also evident that Dr. Cassidy was able to rebuild his medical practice. One letter actually refers to the hundredth baby he had delivered since the end of the war.

A document search at the Rockingham County courthouse in Harrisonburg failed to uncover any official information related to James Christopher "Jamie" Lockhart aside from his birth record. However, a fleeting reference to Dr. Cassidy's "son" in one of the aforementioned letters led my researcher to Washington College (now Washington and Lee) in Lexington, Virginia.

According to the college's admission records, James Christopher Lockhart enrolled as a freshman at that institution in the fall of 1865, the first semester after General Robert E. Lee joined the college as its first postwar president. Mr. Lockhart was then just sixteen years old. His subsequent academic career was auspicious.

Although President Lee wrote no memoirs before his untimely death in 1870 at the age of sixty-three, he was a prolific correspondent. In one letter to John W. Brockenbrough dated March 14, 1866, he states that "the college is blessed with an abundance of highly-motivated and gifted students. Perhaps, foremost among them at the present time is a young man named Lockhart, who could as easily be teaching our courses in English Literature as taking them for credit."

It was during his first year in Lexington that Mr. Lockhart and Katharine Dandridge apparently fulfilled their commitment to the dying "William" La Frenière. From amongst the papers of Frederick Douglass that are still catalogued at the noted abolitionist's last home in Anacostia, D.C., I found an important piece of information while examining a daybook in which Mr. Douglass recorded his appointments. It was also his custom to make brief notes about visitors who aroused his interest and about whom he expected to write further in his journals.

On May 8, 1866, he wrote, "Today I finally received word about two of our operatives, Father James Donaldson of Georgetown and the legendary slave-stealer William, who disappeared without trace in the final days of the war. It is an astounding story that these two young people tell, and one I am inclined to believe, if only for their earnest desire to keep a promise to a dying man. More in my journal."

The name Dandridge appears next to that entry. Unfortunately, there is no surviving record of Mr. Douglass's daily journals from 1866 through 1871. They were destroyed in the fire that consumed the rear quarter of the house in which he was then living at 316 A Street NE, in the District.

Much of what is conclusively known about the life of Katharine Dandridge following the events in the previous narrative can be found in the papers of Helen Drummond Kerfoot, which are now the property of the Virginia Historical Society, and catalogued under the title "Correspondence of a Valley Widow, 1861–1869."

During the fever epidemic that swept away hundreds of citizens of Richmond in the last weeks of the war, Miss Dandridge worked as a volunteer nurse at the makeshift hospital set up by the Baptist Theological Seminary on Duke Street. According to a letter from Mrs. Vaughn Starling to Helen Kerfoot, dated March 2, 1865, she contracted the fever in late January, and was in recuperation at her aunt's home on Franklin Street until June 5, 1865.

Upon regaining her health, Kate apparently returned to her ancestral home near Luray, Virginia, living there for almost two years. According to an auction notice found in the *Page County Dispatch,* the Dandridge family estate was sold at public auction on April 9, 1867.

Based on numerous references in the Kerfoot correspondence, we know that Miss Dandridge and her surviving brother, Robert, left Richmond later that year on a ship bound for San Francisco, California. It was to be the first stop on a year-long trip in which the pair decided to circumnavigate the globe. In a letter written at about the time of their departure, Mrs. Kerfoot cites the determination of Miss Dandridge to find a "new passage" in her life.

The first leg of their tour carried them across the Pacific to Tahiti. Over the next eighteen months, letters from Miss Dandridge to Mrs. Kerfoot arrived from Shanghai, Nepal, and Bombay. Although they include vivid descriptions of the things she saw, there is nothing of a personal nature until her brother Robert became seriously ill in India. Clearly afraid for his life, she accompanied him to the famous sanatorium Castello Mariani in the Tuscany region of Italy, where she remained until he was again well enough to travel.

On June 16, 1869, James Christopher "Jamie" Lockhart graduated with honors from Washington College in Lexington, Virginia. Chosen by President Lee to deliver the valedictory address, he gave a speech that was "very affecting and well-spoken," according to a chronicler in the journal of the college's Diagnothian Literary Society. No written record of the speech exists, although a photograph of Mr. Lockhart standing next to President Lee on the graduation platform can be found in the Washington College Library's Brooke Lewis collection of glass plate negatives. It is interesting to note that based on the known height of Robert E. Lee, Mr. Lockhart had by then grown to stand at least six feet tall. A brief follow-up article in the *Lexington Gazette* reported that Mr. Lockhart was planning to join the faculty of Washington College as its youngest instructor.

During that same summer of 1869, Miss Dandridge and her brother Robert arrived in London, where they were welcomed to the Devonshire estate of Sir Hugh Mercer, a blood relative of Miss Dandridge's mother, and a barrister of some note at that time. A letter from Miss Dandridge to Helen Drummond Kerfoot indicates that his firm of solicitors represented the House of Windsor in many of its family dealings abroad. This may have been the last letter between them. Mrs. Kerfoot succumbed to death by natural causes at her home in Page County in August of that year.

The fall social season in London provided the occasion for Miss Dandridge's formal presentation at Buckingham Palace, and it was memorable enough to merit several paragraphs in Lord Blakenthorpe's *Life and Times of the Court of Queen Victoria* (1861–1901).

In a departure from what is otherwise a dull recital of seemingly endless court functions, he wrote that "her stunning green eyes, auburn hair and slim voluptuous figure made an immediate impression on the Queen. However it was the young Virginia woman's bold and frank opinions that truly captivated Her Royal Highness and caused her to publicly announce to the court that she was henceforth 'adopting' Miss Dandridge during the remainder of her stay in Great Britain."

That same September, James Lockhart became an instructor on the faculty of Washington College, teaching three different humanities courses to the school's rapidly expanding student body. With many Confederate veterans still entering college for the first time, there is no doubt that he was significantly younger than many of his students. This may explain the familiarity of the following reference from one relatively ancient freshman who wrote in his diary, "Jamie can bring the Greeks so alive in the classroom, it is almost like being there."

If there was any correspondence between Miss Dandridge and Mr. Lockhart during this time, there was no reference to it in the letters she wrote to Mrs. Kerfoot. However, in May of 1870, an event occurred in London that seems to confirm that they had indeed remained in contact.

Because of the notoriety of the affair, it was chronicled in virtually every London newspaper. According to the May 7 issue of the *Tatler,* the incident involved two particularly ardent suitors of Katharine Dandridge.

While dining at the Guard's Club, Lord Cantlemere, then one of the richest men in England, allegedly made a statement to his companions regarding what he believed to be his favorable prospects for the marriage. Colonel Dorian St. George Bond, an officer of the Grenadier Guards, was seated at a nearby table and apparently overheard the remark. When Bond confronted Cantlemere with what he charged was a "damnable lie," the two men almost came to blows before being dragged apart. Later that night, Bond sent His Lordship a personal note demanding satisfaction. At dawn the following morning, the two men dueled with pistols on the plain of Hampstead Heath.

Cantlemere was killed instantly by a ball to the brain. St. George Bond was himself mortally wounded, finally succumbing from a stomach wound on the third day after their meeting. In response to an outcry from the London press establishment, Sir Hugh Mercer spoke in fervent defense of Miss Dandridge's character, saying at one point, "She in no way encouraged the aspirations of either gentleman."

The British public was not in a forgiving mood. One newspaper ran an editorial referring to her as a "beguiling temptress" and condemned her actions in "precipitating the murder of two of England's preeminent men." It is important to note that there does not appear to have been any defense of her by a member of the royal family. Virtually shunned by British society, she reportedly left the country with her brother Robert on a packet boat to France in June 1870. There is no record in any of the English publications that covered the "Dandridge Affair" as to what her final destination might have been.

Interestingly, James Lockhart abruptly resigned from his post at Washington College on June 10, 1870, just one week before the end of the spring term. There is no official explanation for his resignation to be found in the college files. The specificity of the date is due entirely to an entry from the same student diarist quoted earlier, who wrote, "Jamie Lockhart apparently surrendered yesterday to the siren of his wanderlust. No one seems to know where he has gone."

It is interesting to speculate that the reason for his sudden departure might have had something to do with the flight of Katharine Dandridge from England. Unfortunately, we have found no evidence to prove it.

In fact, it is here that the trail runs cold for both of them, although not for lack of trying to follow it. For example, my researcher was able to locate three direct descendants of Sir Hugh Mercer who still reside in Devonshire, England. None of them, however, was able to provide us with any new information about Katharine Dandridge or where she might have gone. All efforts to track the movement of Mr. Lockhart were equally fruitless. Any papers or letters that might have been saved by his mother have long since been lost.

There is no record of either of them ever returning to Virginia. A review of the 1880 and 1890 census records show no individuals with their names and ages living in the state.

I am indebted to the librarians at Washington and Lee, who steadfastly reviewed every alumni directory and reunion journal until the year 1925, hoping to find some reference to a Lockhart sighting or even mention of his death.

As is the case with so many other uncelebrated Americans, they simply vanished into the vast world stage. Perhaps new information in the form of letters or journals will someday emerge to shed light on the subsequent lives of these two remarkable young people. Persons who come into possession of such information are invited to contact me.

Acknowledgments

I WOULD LIKE to thank Peter Wolverton, my editor at St. Martin's, whose unerringly fine judgment has made this a better book. A thank-you as well to Julian Muller, a genuine man of letters who was kind enough to share his wisdom along the way.

Finally, I owe a significant debt to Henry Kyd Douglas and Richard Taylor, whose wonderful reminiscences of the Civil War and the Shenandoah Valley inspired so many of us to study that part of the conflict.

Winchester

Valley Pike

MASSANUTTEN RANGE

New Market

Luray

Pinna

Dandridge

Lacey Spring

Trumbo's Tavern

Harrisonburg

Port
Republic

MOUNT

BLUE RIDGE

M. HOLMER 98